W9-CQY-221

9/02   2/03   8/   6/04

Palo Alto City Library

The individual borrower is responsible for all library material borrowed on his or her card.

Charges as determined by the CITY OF PALO ALTO will be assessed for each overdue item.

Damaged or non-returned property will be billed to the individual borrower by the CITY OF PALO ALTO.

P.O. Box 10250, Palo Alto, CA 94303

A Compendium of Skirts

Phyllis Moore

CARROLL & GRAF PUBLISHERS
NEW YORK

For Barbara Hamby, with all my heart

A Compendium of Skirts

Carroll & Graf Publishers
An Imprint of Avalon Publishing Group Inc.
161 William St., 16th Floor
New York, NY 10038

Copyright © 2002 by Phyllis Moore

First Carroll & Graf edition 2002

Interior design by Sue Canavan

Library of Congress Cataloging-in-Publication Data is available.

ISBN: 0-7867-0989-8

Printed in the United States of America
Distributed by Publishers Group West

"Dark but excessive bright thy skirts appear."

—*Paradise Lost*

Contents

❋ ❋ ❋

Acknowledgments

I am thankful to Noah Lukeman, my agent, to Tina Pohlman, the editor, and to Nate Knaebel and copy editor Janet H. Baker, for their grace, generosity, and smarts. Grateful acknowledgment goes to the Illinois Arts Council for help in funding this work. Many thanks to my daytime family: Julia Stibolt, Lorenzo Bracy, and Julie Walner. And I'd like to thank my students, who were always my best teachers. Most of all, thanks to my dear family and friends: Patrick and Yanou Beggs, Kathleen Connolly, Bobbie Epting, Marsha Hosack, Michael Keller, Howard Hudson Moore, Steve and Carolyn Moore, Eddie Quigg, my wise lamb Hannah Racine Shaw, Ken Shaw, Jerry Stern, Gloria Walther and Jeffrey Clayton Walther, and my mother, Rita Moore, for her intelligence, her joie de vivre, and her abiding whimsy, and for whom I will be forever thankful.

"The Language Event" was published in *Redbook* as "Can You See My Brother Smile?" "Once, in Hamburg" appeared in *Apalachee Quarterly,* was reprinted in a special Chicago/Vienna edition of *Another Chicago Magazine,* and cited in the Pushcart Prize anthology. "A Compendium of Skirts" was published in the *Mississippi Review* and cited in *Best American Short Stories.* "Redlight" was published in the *Mississippi Review.* And "Rembrandt's Bones" appeared in the *Georgia Review.*

The Language Event

I had not seen my brother Richard since high school. In sixteen years I'd heard from him twice, once when our Air Force dad died and once from jail. ("Penny-ante shit, kid. Two hunnerd dollars, see your way clear. You know any lawyer? Bring me a shirt.") Then last week out of the blue, he calls to see if I want to go with him to the Indy 500. He says we can meet in Bunker Hill at the bar, then drive on down together. He says he wants to get to know his baby sister. When I ask for the address he tells me,

"Kid. It ain't but only one bar in Bunker Hill."

I made arrangements. The cats, the clients, my hyacinth beds. I even made up a batch of the coconut curry dish the neighbor lady who takes care of my cat likes so much—left it in the refrigerator as a surprise. I rented a car, a Chrysler, the environment be damned, and canceled all and every obligation, even the feisty Mrs.

Gilsinger. I made a special trip out to the only good record store in town for Hoagy Carmichael, the Smithsonian collection, a perfect boxed set. Hoagy Carmichael: the saddest man in the history of Indiana, with the one exception of my brother Richard.

I drove a hundred miles, his thin hurt rounding slow on tinsel cassette tape.

Pool balls click velvet. A dime slides down the jukebox throat.

Voice at the bar: "Reason the dinosaurs gone extinct, they run out of stick."

The only light is the beer light. Tiny Clydesdales run soft and silent around a yellowed Anheuser citadel. It is a roomful of men. The Leaning Men, I think, taking a cautious look around. Rough Giacomettis with eyes worn all the way down to the clay. Men leaning over other men, two over the jukebox, Wurlitzer blue, one over the pinball, others over pool tables, game tables. Over things you put money in and get something in return.

"Reason the dinosaurs gone extinct, sticks gone soft. Sticks gone soft account of equal right. Account of the lady dinosaur equal right."

He said Thursday and this is Thursday. He said noon and it's been noon for an hour. I take another look at my watch.

"Lady dinosaur, she want on top. Lady dinosaur, she big as hell. She want to crush the man."

The bartender looks up from his work. He is grilling rinds from skinny pigs, raised on his own place, just down the road.

I take a deep breath and realize two things. A, my brother is not coming, and B, I am wearing too much perfume.

My brother is not coming because he is in some kind of trouble. Richard was always in some kind of trouble. Once it was a motorcycle and once it was his football coach. Once it was something he said about the government to his civics teacher, a retired master sergeant. The day he lost his base ID card, I thought our Air Force dad would beat him bloody. The announcement came that night at the supper table: Thanks to my brother Richard, the Communists would now be able to take over Indiana.

Meanwhile here I sit, perched on a bar stool in the middle of Nowhere, USA, wearing a festive neck scarf, all tied up in a pretty pink bow and braced to play the female version of Ned Beatty in *Deliverance* to a bar full of what look to be cousins.

"Mary Louise."

It was him.

I got up off the bar stool and spread my arms wide. It was like trying to hug a refrigerator.

"Hey, squirt," he said.

"Hey, yourself," I said.

I squeeze hard, trying to bring back the whole Cheerios-and-milk routine. I step back to take a good long look.

Next to my brother stands a woman with a ponytail.

"This is Red."

Next to the woman stands a beard.

"This is Chit."

The beard raises its head in short incremental jerks as if hoisted on an invisible tire jack. It inches up me, notch by notch, finding absolutely nothing of interest, then down, collapsing back into its original give-up position. The beard is wearing a cap. The cap says EAT MORE PUSSY.

I've had worse dates. I dated a little mountaineer once. He punctuated his sentences and some of his romantic efforts with a little "Ho-o," the way Ed McMahon used to say. For six months I dated a dead man. Finally, he told me. "Sorry. Just dead I guess."

I look at my date.

"Pleased to meet you," I say.

"Pleased to meet you," he says, extending a hand.

His hand is a wadded-up ball of tin foil, small, like a cat toy.

The four of us stand there, an unpracticed quartet.

"Ready to roll?" says Richard.

"Can do!" I say.

He smiles to acknowledge the family joke, but there is a distant look in my brother's terminally green eyes.

Bunker Hill Air Force Base, now Grissom, was a SAC base, and in 1962 everything was in high gear for the upcoming show with Cuba. A Catholic was President. The base was on twenty-four-hour alert.

Crest had been shown to be an effective decay-preventative dentifrice that could be of significant value if used in a conscientiously applied program of oral hygiene and regular professional care. Mary Louise Stinson was eight years old, hell-bent on memorizing anything that got in her path. Sunday next, Psalms 23. There was a new Easter muff in this for her. Somehow between her supper-troubled mom, Jesus, and the deep blue sea, she was going to get that muff. Sheila Daghita could eat dirt and Mary Louise would stand over her and watch. White virgin rabbit fur, lined in silk-white satin. In the presence of mine enemies.

Castro was only a word.

Bunker Hill Air Force Base was the place to be in 1962. They had one of the Doomsday planes. The other one was in Nebraska, a place too distant to count. The Doomsday plane was for the President for when the end of the world came. Even an eight-year-old could appreciate the glamour of living where the President of the United States and his wife might come when the world blew up. Thy rod and thy staff, they comfort me.

Their father worked on the flight line, NCO. His squadron's motto was CAN DO! This message echoed relentlessly throughout the house—on mounted plaques, on coffee cup coasters, the welcome mat. It rang in Mary Louise's ears night and day. It was in the green beans they ate for supper every night, cold and thin, spooned straight out of the can.

On top of the TV set there lived a little ceramic family of ducks. Three baby ducks with Mama foremost. They were strung together by a cheap brass chain. Mama Duck always looked a little tired to Mary Louise, a little jumpy. But bold across her breast were the words tattooed in gold: CAN DO!

The top drawer of their father's dresser drawers was his sock drawer. You had to make his socks smile. The three of them lined up behind his six-foot-tall fatigues—Mary Louise, her brother Richard, and their little blonde mom.

First, match pairs. Put the one on top of his buddy and press down hard. Italy, see? Now roll up from the toes. Jelly roll, see? Take this one's lip, pull it tight, all the way around, turn him face up, pinch up the sides of his mouth. See him smile?

"When I open my sock drawer," their father said, "I don't want to see anything but smiles."

"*Can do, Dad!*" they said.

There was a fan in the living room; it was a fan for jets.

Their father brought it home from the flight line—it cooled the whole house off, top to bottom. It stood up in the corner of the living room like a man. Once, Ricky took her kitten, a black Manx named Blackie, held it up in front of the fan, and let go. The kitten actually flew a foot or so, then dropped easily into the crystal ashtray on the coffee table.

"It's women."

The four of us were spread out picnic-style—Richard, his girlfriend Red, me, my date.

"They can really fuck you up."

Soon a thematic thread emerged. Seems Chit's whole life, women had really fucked him up. First, his mother. She dies early in the story though, bad conscience you bet, and life begins to look up for little Chit. It was just him and Pete.

"Who's Pete?" I ask.

"Pete's my dad," says Chit, surprised at my inability to follow such a simple narrative line.

Things could not be better for father and son. They fished, played catch, smoked dope. It was as Ward-and-Beaver as it gets, recounted Chit. Until one Monday morning after a trip to Kansas City, Pete comes home with Chit's new stepmother.

"She really fucked me up."

The stepmother emerges as a kind of cross between

Muammar al-Qaddafi and Cruella De Vil, a well-heeled terrorist in a Disney sports coupe. A step can fuck you up, according to Chit, worse than your own blood. Next, high school. Chit falls in love. Never in his life had he met anyone quite like Cindy, but in the end,

"She fucked me up royal."

He drops out of school and travels around the state awhile till he lands a job just outside of Kokomo. Melting down iron ore gives Chit a kind of satisfaction he has never known. There was this woman. And before he knew what hit him, he was married, childed, cheat upon, childed again, this time not even his, and kicked clean out of their little brown house before you could say squat-diggity-dog—kicked out, by the way, of a house which now belongs to the tramp and her lawyer.

"She fucked me up but good."

There was a poem on Chit's T-shirt. It was too long to memorize but the gist of it was: my old lady might not think much of its size, but once I get her turned over, this old pal of mine starts looking real big. The word *wicket* figured prominently in the rhyme scheme.

"Women," concluded Chit, wishing things were otherwise.

He looked to Richard for support. Richard was playing with my key chain. I have a million keys. Car keys, house keys, front door, back door, side, and porch. Keys for the office, keys for the garage, keys that open I don't know what. My brother had been listening to Chit, but he was looking at me. He said,

"Are you important?"

We were parked in front of Hooker's Hamburgers, squashed in between hundreds of other campers lining both sides of the highway leading up to the Speedway. It cost a hundred and fifty dollars to park.

"These boys don't take American Express," Richard said, as I pulled out my American Express.

My brother's camper was a great lumbering pachyderm, one of the first RVs off the assembly line. It came about an inch off the ground. Richard and Chit had gone in on it together. They pooled their money, their carburetor skills, their Saturdays off. When it was all fixed up and running, they painted it pink. It was a pink an eight-year-old girl with high self-esteem would pick out.

"He did the left, I did the right," said Chit.

"Looks nice," I said.

There wasn't an inch of space left in all of Indiana. Still, they came: eight lanes of highway fat with cars, trucks, campers, and vans. Teenage cars souped up in the back like cats in heat; mean-spirited trucks angry for a place to park; friendlier station wagons, tailgates open, swinging legs and tossing out free beers and tokes. Race fans galore arriving by the minute from nowhere to here, spilling out onto the pavement like excited crickets, like the scene at the end of *Day of the Locusts,* the movie about Hollywood and alienation where the one small lonely guy gets swallowed up whole by the mindless masses. Dark little movie, that. But this was no movie. This was Indiana.

It was a day of celebration. Everyone had come in their best descriptive wear. There were T-shirts of saddened commentary (SHIT HAPPENS), T-shirts of regret (TOO DRUNK TO FUCK), and T-shirts of directive (GIVE ME HEAD TILL I'M DEAD). Apparently, all these people ordered out of the same catalog.

And the refrain, *"Show us your tits! Show us your tits!",* a chant you could hear repeated in the distance and see printed on signage—on upturned cases of beer sitting friendly by the side of the road; on the sides of cars, spray-painted in red. It was written on makeshift cardboard signs necklacing entire gangs of boy drunks running hither and thither, Polaroids dangling:

"Show us your tits! Show us your tits!"

Perhaps this is what historian Paul Fussell meant in his essay on the subject in which he described the Indy 500 as "a language event." He found the entire experience "therapeutic." Of course, his point of reference was World War I.

Before leaving Chicago, I had taken the time to read up on the Indy 500 in order to acquaint myself with the nature of auto racing. For weeks now I'd been keeping up with the sports sections of the two daily papers, familiarizing myself with the names of the drivers, their sponsors, the preferred motor oil. I memorized the mph of all thirty-three qualifying cars. I rehearsed things to say.

"Som-a-bitch. Can't do more'n two-thirteen. And that's in the stretch." This I would say to my brother in the conversation we would have about the aging A. J. Foyt. He would look at me, appreciative, and smile.

"Fifty-seven years old, though, sis. You got to love the guy."

I would try out my Chevrolet joke.

"Ask me, Heartbeat of America barely has a pulse."

I would deliver this line slow, lean back on my left elbow, and pull out my smokes. First, the lighter. I'd tap my Marlboro on the silver surface of my cigarette lighter, packing the tobacco the way our father used to do. The lighter would be a real lighter, the kind you have to put fluid in, not one of those pansy-ass throwaway Bics. There's a little white pad on the bottom you have to soak.

And we would smoke, my brother and I, smoke the whole day away, nothing else. Ricky would turn to me at some point: "Hey, sis. Out of smokes."

And I would look up lazy into that Indiana sky, inhale all the way down like Claudette Colbert, and breathe out slow.

"Look in my purse."

This is what I would say to my brother.

It was hot. Only Indiana knows how to be this hot. Digging in my purse I find my toothpaste warm.

No one was saying a word. It was as if we had all forgotten the language. Chit was taking a breather from his life story and Richard had his head on Red's bare stomach. They were tangled in a way I felt I could not intrude upon. The little pink reunion I had acted out in my mind between me and my brother had not happened and would not unless I did something, so when Ricky stood up and walked over to the beer cooler I said,

"Howdy Hughes to win."

Ricky stood up straight and stretched and then looked slow down into the crowd.

"He only clocked two-o-two in nine, I'll grant you that, but Ricky. Guess his sponsor."

He turned around and reached deep down into the cooler.

"He's no speedster, so okay. But guess who his sponsor is. Take one guess."

"Beer?" he said.

"I'm fine," I said.

"It was the night before Christmas."

It was the night before Christmas, and Chit was on a

plane to Vegas when he made the mistake of doing the tequila first.

"Beer first," he said. "It coats the stomach."

Problem. The guy beside him in the aisle seat was asleep. Chit, on his way to "puke up all eighteen dollars' worth of airplane tequila," could not step over the guy. He didn't want to wake him up. Poor guy looked like he could use the sleep. Probably some woman had fucked him up. So he decided on the next best route in order to be polite. He sat back down in his seat, retrieved one of the empties, took aim, and successfully fired every single red cent of his sickness back into the empty beer can in his hand.

"That hole on top a beer can," bragged Chit. "Mighty small."

"About the size of your johnson."

It was Red. She had finished painting her toenails red and was now taking a brush to her ponytail. Head down, she swatted it hard, as if it were a mischievous child.

Red was everything I wasn't. She was good looking, and she did not feel the need to apologize. She was intelligent, and she did not feel the need to apologize. She threw back her head, faced the full Indiana sun, and with one expert flick of the wrist, she twisted the rope of hair into the most beautiful ponytail the world has ever known.

It hung down her back like a beautiful red question mark.

"Jiffy Mix," I said.

"Why you went in the first place is all I want to know." My best friend Marsha was sautéing scallops. "What on earth did you think you were going to prove?"

"I don't know. I'm not just the Queen of Comet and he's not just a redneck drunk?"

"So?"

"So. I'm the Queen of Comet and he's a redneck drunk."

"Don't Oprah me."

"I know."

"If I hear that story about making your father's socks smile one more time—"

"I know."

"Look, kiddo. My father wasn't born with a naturally sunny disposition either, you know."

"I know."

"What do you want for Christmas this year? I'm thinking gravy boat."

I realized then I could never tell even my best friend about the meal Ricky made me. Marsha clarifies butter just to make a scrambled egg.

The day my brother Richard ruined his life by getting the

head cheerleader pregnant was the day he forgot to make our father's socks smile. Our father had just returned home off of TDY in the Philippines. It was the day he brought home the wood spoon.

All Air Force families grow up with the same household items. You start out with the velvet tapestry of the Lord's Supper. You hang that in the dining room over the teakwood dining table, cheap from Sweden. You hang the big wood fork from the Philippines to the left of the Lord's Supper, and the spoon the size of a man to the right. Forks to the left, spoons to the right. It's a natural military tropism.

In the living room goes the father's chair, the center of gravity. There's a switch on the bottom you flick on to make it vibrate. In front of the chair goes the camel-saddle stool from Saudi Arabia. This is where the feet go when *The Huntley-Brinkley Report* is on. To the left you put the ceramic elephant from Iraq. This is where the cat sleeps. If you don't have a cat, this is where the *Reader's Digest*s go. After dinner you put the coffee cup on the TV-tray table to the right of the father's chair. The coffee cup goes on the coffee cup coaster. It's from Holland. There's a picture of a little blue windmill on it.

Because her family was the last family on Bunker Hill Air Force Base to get the big spoon, for Mary Louise this was a red-letter day. She was up on the stepladder helping her mother hang the spoon when she heard their father.

He had opened his sock drawer and, to his dismay, one of his little black sock battalions was not smiling. Ricky would have to be taught a lesson.

After, Mary Louise knew where to find her brother. It was 1962 and he was just seventeen. He was in the carport doing something on his beloved 1957 Chevy. She stood quiet in the doorway and waited for him to see her.

He saw her. He was putting polish on the things over the wheels.

He said, "You can help do the skirts."

It was late now. The four of us had settled into a kind of life atop the camper. We had a blanket spread out, battened down by our four selves, one at each corner, like eternally bored dragons on a no-century map of the world. Chit had chosen the poet's corner, the corner closest to the beer cooler upon which he rested his head, weary from having to keep up the conversation for the whole group, exhausted from having depleted his generous supply of pussy, poontang, and puke tales. My brother was curled up in a gentle Indiana nap. Red was reading a historical novel on the life of Anne Boleyn, hardback. Left to my own devices, I did what I do best under pressure. I shopped; in this case, the sky.

It was a Victoria's Secret sky. All afternoon long, ladies' bras had been flying through the air like kites, perforating the lacy Indiana sky. I critiqued each one, sorting by shape,

material, front or back closure, probable uplift and price.
I ordered out of Victoria's Secret once but wound up
sending it back. It was a red bra with tulip-shaped cups
and wide-set straps. There was a bit of a balcony on it, the
kind of French I like, but all in all it was just not me.

And as I was thinking this, and thinking maybe I
shouldn't have sent it back, the most logical thing in the
world happened.

"Show us your tits! Show us your tits!"

When you see a dead animal in the road at a great distance on a cross-country drive, and you say to yourself,
Calm down, it's okay, it's not a dead animal in the road,
it's only a tire; and then you get closer and closer and you
know it is *not* only a tire but is *indeed* a dead animal in
the road, you will know what it was to look down into
the eyes of a hundred beer-stunned boy drunks, Polaroids
cocked, who at that moment surrounded our camper.

"Show us your tits! Show us your tits!"

It was a dead animal in the road.

I tucked my legs up under. "Richard?" I said, but he
remained sound asleep. I looked at Red. She turned a
page. Anne Boleyn was in a lot of hot water. I looked at
my date, my own darling, and I have to say I was a little
hurt. He looked as if nothing could be less interesting to
him personally than me showing my tits. I looked down
into the sea of sunny faces below, lit yellow with beer and
cheap desire.

"Sorry, boys, not my idiom."

It was a thought more than a statement.

They got quiet. They were thinking. I was kidding, right? I was from out of state, right?

"Show us your tits! Show us your tits!"

Somebody threw a full can of beer. Cold metal grazed the side of my head. Then there was a noise behind me.

It was Red. She started out with a little scooting dance. It was not the parading of a cheap showgirl but performed with a kind of so-what that was perfectly Indiana. Her arm swings were not as fluid as they could have been, but then again Red probably didn't have the advantage of Madame Assouline for six summers of ballet. (It's all in the ankles, she told me later.) After a few noiseless turns, she crossed her arms over her in front, and with all the grace of the Queen of the Nile she began to inch her T-shirt up. Days passed. One boy, a carrottop of maybe fifteen, stepped on the front bumper and began to climb his way up, but Chit, thinking quickly, poured his beer down the front of the camper so the boy slid down to the ground.

Red was good. She looked as if she had been stripping for hoodlum boy drunks her entire red and lovely life. She turned now, her back to them, and began to tease the hook of her bra. This drove the crowd completely out of their minds. Apparently, none of these people get cable. Then, with the ease of a professional aerialist accustomed to such minor displays, she twirled one last splendiferous twirl and flung her bra into the wild Indianapolis air.

It was the red tulip-shaped bra from Victoria's Secret.

I watched as it hung in the air for one long moment, and then dropped softly down into the crowd, like a kitten.

And I couldn't help but look. Red's breasts were the most intelligent breasts I had ever seen. They were small and hard and undeniable. They said, Go ahead, take your time. They said, Go on, look all you want. Get you an eyeful. They're mine and I like them. Red turned to Chit:

"Look in my purse."

She took paper and pen, wrote something down.

"You boys ever heard of equal right?"

She held her makeshift sign up to the crowd. It said:

Show us your dicks! Show us your dicks!

And they did.

Richard stood up. The sight of so many dicks seemed to have an effect on him.

It took eight state troopers to clear the crowd. One trooper pointed straight up at me and shouted, "We're hauling all y'alls asses to jail."

I considered this new possibility. A, jail would be indoors, B, jail would have food, and C, jail would not have hoodlum boy drunks demanding I show them my tits.

The jail would be like the jail on *The Andy Griffith Show*—friendly and, above all, temporary. Aunt Bee would bring us supper in a big wicker basket covered with a starched white linen napkin. Maybe Andy wouldn't even bother locking us up. We could come and go just like Otis. Ricky and I would talk, really talk, really get to know each other, see what made each other tick. I would finally get to tell my brother what I had come here to tell him. That I was sorry. Sorry his life had been so hard while mine had been so easy. Sorry that, in our family, I got to be the girl while he had to be the boy.

Midnight in Indianapolis. Tomorrow is the race. I get it now, finally. My brother has not come here for any race. And he has certainly not come for any family reunion. He has come here to get drunk and fuck.

I was alone inside the camper. I had squashed myself into the pull-down bed over the driver's seat. Earlier, when the others left to go closer to the Speedway where they said the real party was, I pretended to be asleep.

I drove a hundred miles for what?

I felt numbed and begrimed and exhausted, numbed by my inability to make a connection with my brother, begrimed by the endless stream of sex-filth allusions, exhausted by trying so hard to be at ease in this, my brother's, world. I did not find it cute that a mean gang of anything-by-the-quart drunks wanted me to show them my tits. I did not think it neat to be set up with a man whose goal in life was to eat more pussy. I did not find the aerodynamics of puking interesting, nor the size of a man's wicket. I did not consider this "a language event." I needed a shower. I needed two showers. Not to mention all I had had to eat all day long was cheap headache beer and a pack of wintergreen Certs, and I was starving. Hooker's Hamburgers does not take American Express.

Most of all I was shamed. The boys were right. Who did I think I was? To sashay into my brother's life, have our little pink reunion just the way I imagined it, all Andy Griffith and sunshine, and return to my sparkling white-wine three o'clock life? Safe—no mess, no stain, no scuff marks. And wouldn't it make a good story? Wouldn't it be interesting to tell friends around the dinner table some night, ladling it out with my most recent hit, a cold walnut pasta salad, about the time my redneck brother took me to the Indy 500?

It was an earthquake.

I grabbed the metal bar that looped around my makeshift bed as the camper began to shake, first a gentle side-to-side and then a violent rocking. My glasses fell off.

"Show us your tits! Show us your tits!"

It was an animal on the side of the road. I locked my left arm around the metal bar and felt around the bed for something, anything, but it was all blanket. This is Indiana, I told myself. Nothing bad ever happens to you in Indiana. These were only boys, and boys get tired and give up and go home and leave you alone because you're the grown-up here. You are over them.

"Bitch! Show us your tits!"

I couldn't remember if I locked the door, and then I remembered I didn't. A dish broke. Someone was inside the camper.

I pulled the blanket around me and shut my eyes as if, if I could not see it happen, it would not happen.

"Mary Louise?"

It was Ricky. He had been here the whole time.

And then my brother did what big brothers do. He stepped out of the camper. And he just stood there. There must have been forty or fifty of them, drunk and stoned and ready to party, but they turned and went when all Ricky said was,

"Go."

He stepped back into the camper, closed the door, retrieved his sister's glasses and asked was she okay. He helped her down from her little makeshift bed and went over to the little camper stove.

"Hungry?" he said.

"You cook?" she said.

"Can do."

He was a big man, her brother. He had the kind of arms that made you want to ask about his life—they were thin and hard-working. They were the arms of a man who had not had the opportunity to live life pretty.

He said, Get the hamburger and she got the hamburger. The refrigerator didn't work so the meat was brown, not just on top so you can peel it off but all the way through. Ricky took out a skillet and put the bad meat in to fry. He told her, Get the beans and she got the beans. It was one of those family-size cans of pork and beans, some off brand, not even Campbell's. He handed her his pocketknife. She worked and worked but was getting nowhere fast so he took the can and the pocketknife from her, gave the can a whack, sawed the knife around, and finished the job.

There was a square piece of cold white fat on top.

"Don't toss that out," he said, as she looked around for some place to toss it out.

He poured the pork and beans into the bad meat frying.

He said, Get the water, and she got the water. It was a dirty plastic milk container they had filled up on the way there from somebody's backyard spigot. There was grass in it. Ricky poured the water, grass and all, into the bad meat frying.

"Sorry, kid," he said, when he saw there was no salt. "Tabasco do?"

"Tabasco's great," she said.

He pulled out a bag of potatoes from under the stove and handed her back his pocketknife. He said Peel, and she peeled. He said Slice, and she sliced. The potatoes were soft and brown all the way through. Put those in, he said, and she put those in.

She set the table. Forks to the left, spoons to the right. It is a natural family tropism. She found two Taco Bell napkins and folded them into little airplanes, and she put those under the forks because that is where they go.

Ricky popped them two beers.

And they ate. Ricky got the idea to put a little beer in his, and his sister followed suit. She did this mainly for sanitation purposes, but she wants you to know. It was good.

And she told him so.

And he said, "Kid. If it's one thing. I can cook."

It was a Neil Sedaka night. A Catholic sat in the White House. Ricky Stinson forgot to make his father's socks smile so he had to be taught a lesson. Afterward, he went and waxed his beautiful 1957 Chevy within an inch of its crocus-yellow life. He drove over to Sherry McInerney's house, head cheerleader, and took her to the drive-in movie. He wasn't thinking about Castro that night, or when the world would finally come to an end. He wasn't thinking surely goodness and mercy shall follow me all the days of my life. There was no Easter muff in this for him. And when you are just seventeen and the son of an Air Force father, when you live on Bunker Hill Air Force Base in Bunker Hill, Indiana, in 1962, you don't get an abortion.

You get married, you move to Indianapolis, you get an address. You sell your beautiful 1957 Chevy. You have a little crooked baby.

And so on.

The Things They Married

First, she married herself. His name was Waldo, and he was everything she had ever wanted. A Buddhist who knew how to cha-cha. A chemical engineer who played the theremin in the subway for free. He had a way with children, waiters, and carburetors and could whistle the *Moonlight Sonata* straight through without a single gasping breath, despite his ruined lungs, permanently scarred in childhood from bout upon bout of baby pneumonia. They met at the city's annual dog show, where both he and she had come separately as spectators, dogless. Waldo threw a white cotton sheet over her head and asked if she could see out. She said yes she could, so he took her hand and led her out of the building, past every poodle, every pug. *Be my ghost,* he proposed. And she accepted. They moved into his place, where his heroin addict girlfriend, Digger, still lived. The three got along together well for a time. Then something began to happen. The bride began to notice, with each and every passing day, that Waldo was becoming more and more like her, his bride. He was becoming herself. Before she knew it, he had become more her than her. He began to wear her clothes. At first just her jeans, but then her tops too, and finally the pink crinoline skirt, her favorite, a thing she reserved for special occasions. The clothes seemed happier now and, truth be told, they looked better on him. They looked as if they had finally found, after an exhaustive search, their rightful owner. So after a while there no longer was any need for her to be her. He was doing that already, and he was doing a pretty good job.

Now there was no one for her to be. She became *not* herself, irritated. First over something; then over nothing; finally, the cotton balls. Every morning, Waldo's bride would wake and go into the bathroom where, on top of the toilet tank, sat four or five used cotton balls, each with its own pinprick of red. The wastepaper basket was just to the right of the tank, not inches away. Now, would that be asking too much? One more inch, and that would be that. Your work here is done! Couldn't you at least, dagblame it, try? In fact, Digger could not. The enormity of the task was too much. So the task became a task for the bride to perform. And she did. Each morning, upon entering the bathroom, she donned a yellow Playtex rubber glove and tossed each blooded cotton ball into the wastebasket. Enter, toss. Enter, toss. The marriage was beginning to sour. Digger now, openly and without apology, referred to the bride as *Waldo's latest acquisition.* Then, on Halloween night, the doorbell rang. The children were at the door, but there was no candy in the house. Everyone, including the bride, had forgotten that tonight was Halloween. Waldo suggested pennies, but in the whole wide house not a penny could be found. So they turned the house lights off and waited for the children to go away. But the children did not go away, and the doorbell kept ringing. The ringing kept ringing. They all three of them thought they might very well go insane. Digger said, I know. She went to the hall closet and brought out a Walgreen's bag and went to the front door where the children were all gathered. Later that night, upon dumping out the contents of their candy bags, each child would find, mixed among the Milky Ways, a gleaming white syringe.

So she married Ned, an arithmetic teacher, and they had a baby, a baby girl, whom they named Algebra. But when they brought the baby home from the hospital, she wouldn't stop crying. And by the time they realized they better get the baby back to the hospital, the baby was in a coma. She died in her hospital crib, six weeks old. Nobody ever told them what went wrong. They asked the doctor. They asked the nurses. An orderly offered a theory. Perhaps the baby was dehydrated. Perhaps the baby had cried too hard and for too long and when that happens, sometimes the baby can—well. They buried Algebra in Rosehill, the biggest cemetery in town. After the funeral, advertisements began to arrive in the mail. The cemetery was having a two-for-one sale. For nine-hundred-odd dollars, a plot could be purchased in their special memory garden, a plot big enough for two. There were rolling hills upon which gracious maples with dappling leaves grew. The offer was tempting. But Ned decided he would rather die out loud, in front of his dead baby's mother, day by day, drip-drip-drip, without the comfort of hills or leaves or trees.

So she married the Red Baron. She took Highway 294 south to Interstate 88 west to I-39 south. She stayed on I-39 for twenty-eight miles, then took Exit 72 to Mendota. It was summer and she felt like taking a long drive, getting out of the city, so she rented a car and took a drive down to Mendota, Illinois, for the Mendota Sweet Corn Fest. She had read about it in the newspaper. There would be a parade with floats, bands, antique and classic autos, Shriners, and more. The Jesse White Tumblers would perform along with the Yasgur's Farm Folk & Rock Band. The Mendota Fire Department was going to put on a demonstration for the children. BRING YOUR CHILDREN TO THE ELKS CLUB PARKING LOT, a flyer said. WE WILL TEACH THEM FIRE

SAFETY PROCEDURES THAT COULD SAVE THEIR LIFE. But what interested her most was the butter. Never, growing up, could she get enough butter, in time, on her corn on the cob. Even when her mother brought home the corn-on-the-cob holders shaped like corn on the cobs, down into which the slathered butter would slide and reside, the problem went unresolved. By the time you got the butter all over the corn, the corn was no longer warm. But at the Mendota Sweet Corn Festival, here's what they did. There were twenty-odd vendors with their own booths. In each booth sat a giant black cauldron of boiling water. Children, running in from the fields, their arms laden with the freshly cut ears, tossed them to the mothers. The mothers ripped off the husks and dropped the corncobs into the cauldrons. Fathers sat over their fires like minutemen. Three minutes and the corn was removed with steaming steel tongs. The mothers now came to the fore, piercing each ear with a sharp-ended wood stick, easy as a kebab. The stick shot all the way through, perfect, like an Iroquois arrow. Then, the dream. Each ear-on-a-stick was tossed into a barrelful of melted butter, waiting warm. The cobs disappeared, deep down into the barrel of gold, and then bobbed back up like apples. The customer could now pick out her own corn from the butter barrel and pay, which is just what she did. She had one, then two, and then three. For the first time in a long time—ever since she could, in fact, remember—the world was exactly everything she had ever wished for it to be.

A little red plane—crop duster, maybe?—had, all afternoon long, been flying low over the crowd. Upon investigation, she discovered you could drive north, out of town, and a mile on your left in an open, plowed cornfield, was a guy giving rides for free. He situated you in the front seat, made sure you were comfortable, and then walked to the front and cranked the engine by giving the propeller a yank, easy as if he were starting a lawn mower. The plane was from the barnstorming years, and his name was Lymon; what was hers? One ride, two rides, three, and they were set. He could tell she was afraid of heights, that she was doing this to scare herself out of something, so he offered her a leather flyer's hat to put on, said to have once been worn by Amelia Earhart. She knew it wasn't true. He was just saying that so she wouldn't be frightened. Struck by the enormity of such a kindness, paid to a stranger, on a kid's ride, in the bright middle of summer, she decided to enjoy herself. In fact, she began to think she had been born to fly, like this, in a red plane over a yellow field in the middle of nowhere special. Winters, they lived in Lymon's grandmother's trailer in New Smyrna Beach. Summers, they flew north for the festivals: the corn in Illinois, the wheat in Kansas, the Iowa green bean. When they landed, it would be her job to walk into town with the ten-gallon gas can and find the station. The gas could be leaded or unleaded, it was up to her. And then after a while, it was completely up to her. And then, suit yourself. So she did. She stopped going to the festivals, preferring to stay in Florida in the trailer and watch TV. Lymon, too, began to suit himself. His grandmother Edith, the town beauty in her day, had died the year before and left behind stacks of newspaper clippings: about Lymon, the Florida Red Baron, which is what he called himself, and other clippings, old and yellowed, from the forties, about her own flight with beauty. She had been voted the 1942 Honey Bee Queen of New Smyrna Beach. One night the trailer caught fire and burned to the ground. A match had been struck, like Madam Woolf says. Unexpectedly, and in the dark.

The bride grew tired of marrying men, so she decided from now on she would only marry things. The first thing she married was a stick. She walked into the woods and searched and searched until she found the perfect walking stick. The stick came from a family of actors. The mother had been Tiny Tim's crutch in the 1951 *Scrooge,* and the father was the walking cane that belonged to Kris Kringle in *Miracle on 34th Street.* The father was last seen standing up, in the corner of the living room in Natalie Wood's dreamhouse, the very thing she had wished for the most.

When the stick gave out, she married a rock. It was of

metamorphic descent, from a family of volcanoes in the Hawaiian Islands, and quickly came apart in her hands, so she married a bee. The bee stings her over and over again, but only because he loves her. He loves this girl, this thing, who, time and time again, refuses, ever, to learn.

Big Pink and
Little Minkie

B ig Pink and Little Minkie get on the number 147 bus every morning at Foster and Sheridan. Two elegant maiden ladies, I'm guessing of Russian descent, in their late seventies, early eighties. Again, I'm guessing. They take the 10:25 A.M. bus downtown, the one I take when I'm late to work—which, these days, is pretty much every day—and then, back home, the 5:06 P.M. When they get on the bus in the evening, they are laden with bags from the most exclusive shops, but unlike other women on the bus who reuse such bags, converting them to pseudo-suitcases in which they carry gym clothes, leftover takeout, and stolen office supplies, Big Pink and Little Minkie's bags are filled with expensive well-chosen items purchased that day at the shops their bags say they came from. Their favorite store is Chanel. They go there at least once a week. I have bags too, but mine're grocery-store bags—perfect for my purposes nonetheless, as their handles rarely break, and in winter you can set them down anywhere on the city slosh because their plastic bottoms won't give out. After ruining not one, not two, but three two-hundred dollar leather bags, I gave up. I do have one good bag, though, at home in the closet, reserved for Mother's visits. The first time she came to Chicago and saw me with those grocery bags—well. *But Mother, all that stuff I have to carry back and forth. Between work and school and all. Books, papers to grade. You know.* Her look shut me up. Three days after her return home to Florida I received in the mail, via UPS Express, one of those ugly Land's End lesbian carryalls, a bag more suitable, in Mother's mind, to my position in life. My position in life is, I am a forty-year-old secretary for a soon-to-be indicted accounting firm. Tuesday and Thursday nights, I teach playwriting at a bad college with a good reputation. I only teach to pay the bills, the tremendous salary allowing me the chance to pursue my dream of some day becoming a career office worker.

I call them Big Pink and Little Minkie because Big Pink is tall and wears a big pink coat and matching pink hat, whereas Little Minkie is little. Her coat is mink, and her hat is mink to match. The two women are best friends, often linking arms the way European schoolgirls do, once they've decided they cannot possibly live

without each other. They are perfect together, a lip-
sticked and manicured Rocky and Bullwinkle, only
wealthy and perhaps a little less likely to find themselves
in sticky and extenuating circumstances on a daily basis.
For if they are moose and squirrel, they are aristocratic
moose and squirrel. They sit always at the front of the
bus, as close to the driver as possible. These are the good
seats, the favored seats, the seats where the king and queen
would go, were the king and queen in town and the royal
carriage in the shop for repairs.

I can never decide which of the two ladies I like more.
Big Pink is handsome at eighty, her posture balletic. Her
mother told her to keep her ears over her shoulders and
that's just what she did. My posture has gone to hell in a
handbasket. Centuries of grading papers in bed and the
obsessive need, since birth, to apologize has rendered me
a hunchback. My only hope is when I reach the age of Big
Pink, my hump fully formed, I'll be able to charge people
to touch it for good luck, as was the practice in small vil-
lages in Italy in medieval times.

On the other hand, Little Minkie is the talker, and I
like a talker. She's the president and CEO of the Idea
Committee, that much is clear—where to have lunch, the
Drake or the Palmer House, which lunchtime lecture or
recital to attend. The organist at the Fourth Presbyterian
is doing Bach at noon, but then, too, it's Mies van der
Rohe Day at the Architecture Foundation. Little Minkie

offers up each idea for her friend's consideration, like a foil-wrapped chocolate. It is Big Pink, though, who has the final say. In this partnership, it is clear who holds the power of the veto.

But Big Pink is not on the bus this morning for some reason, only Little Minkie. She's in her usual spot at the front, arrayed in all her sweet mink, as usual. She looks exactly as she does every day: gloves, lipstick, handkerchief somewhere, no doubt. It *is* Christmas Eve. Maybe her friend is home getting the house ready for the evening's festivities, though it's hard to picture Big Pink stringing cranberry necklaces, much less popcorn, for the tree. I could see her instructing a serf how to do it, she has that royal air of command in her bearing. I imagine their life together is a very orderly routine, pleasing to both. A French provincial sideboard in the entryway with a small vase of fresh flowers. When they come home in the evening, they set their mail and their keys on this table while they put their hats on hooks and their coats on hangers in the hall closet and then take their Chanel packages to their respective bedrooms. They get real mail, real letters, addressed in beautiful cursive Russian lettering. I think they have a sister back in Russia who did not come over. They look sometimes as if they're missing someone. They may have had husbands, but I don't think so. It's a sister, younger, married with a new baby, who just did not have the courage to board that ship. Big Pink likes to take a long bath as soon as she gets home, to warm herself up. The bathtub is a big white porcelain one with lion-claw feet. She takes an ancient pharmaceutical bottle from the medicine cabinet and taps into the bathwater a very few drops of the Arabian myrrh she's kept all these years, a gift from a lover. The fragrant drops remind her of the teenage winter she spent once in Italy. So many sights. So many shoes. She had never been exposed to profusion of any kind. It left her giddy and generous for a time, until she returned back home to her former life of teacups.

While Pink is taking a bath, Minkie sets up the samovar, placing it on the glass coffee table in the living room—okay, mahogany. She returns to the kitchen to make something elegant with a potato. Minkie likes to listen to Tchaikovsky when she cooks. She hears in the music the sleigh bells of her drinking uncle's horse-drawn carriage, and it makes her happy to think of him and his little runt son, her cousin, who never did learn how to spell. After dinner, Big Pink and Little Minkie get into quilted robes, flowered and full-length, with handsome silk collars, and they rest on the couch and read. They have a TV, but there is only one show they really like and that doesn't come on until very late in the evening, plus they're all reruns now. *Matlock,* Minkie is happy to read in *People* magazine, was Greta Garbo's favorite TV show too. They read on the couch for hours, that crimson-silk high-backed sofa, Minkie on the left and Big Pink on the right. Minkie likes to read magazines, the *National Geographic* being her favorite, while Pink just reads *Anna Karenina* over and over and over. Halfway through the text for the umpteenth time, she comes across her favorite passage and smiles.

Minkie looks up. *Go ahead, dear, read it out loud. I never get tired of hearing it.*

Happiness, says her lovely elegant friend, eyeglasses sliding down the intelligent nose, *is not the fulfillment of one's desires.*

It most certainly is not, says Minkie, raising her head and looking at her good friend with the exact amount of appreciation the moment requires, then returning to her article on pandas.

The bus comes to a complete standstill. It's a sunshine delay.

When I first moved to Chicago and heard the term *sunshine delay,* my ears blinked. A sunshine delay is a traffic jam caused by an event they call sun. Drivers slow their cars to a halt because they cannot see. They become blind, like ground moles. The glint off their windshields takes them aback. What can it be? What is that big round light in the sky? I took the El the first year I moved to Chicago, which, once you get downtown, takes you underground. But I soon discovered I was living in caveland, where nine months out of the year there is cloud cover. It gets so dark so early that at three o'clock in the afternoon the neighborhood streetlights come on. We have sunshine delays in Tallahassee too, where I come from, but in Tallahassee we call a sunshine delay *night*. It is always 8:30 at night in Chicago. The gloom such a continual moody darkness generates resulted in my painting the entire apartment popsicle orange, the color of Nehi, a shade of orange kids and actors adore but grown-ups find a little difficult to take seriously. I made a New Year's resolution: Stay above the earth. I stopped taking the El and bought a bus pass. I have been taking the number 147 bus now for three years. It is like having a chauffeured limousine, but only a buck fifty a ride. I can get home from work in twenty minutes, while the same trip by El or car would take at least an hour. Some riders call it the Seven-forty-seven, because it is an express bus and flies down Lake Shore Drive. But this morning, because of the sunshine delay, Lake Shore Drive is a parking lot.

It is the day before Christmas and the bus is full. There are holiday out-of-towners, dressed up for a day at the museum, a date with a dinosaur and then lunch at the Walnut Room with their crazy Yankee aunt. There are a few of the surly ones, resentful to have to work on the twenty-fourth, and some of the regulars. The Boyfriend Historian with her hidden cell-phone hookup, for instance. I thought she was a schizophrenic until I saw the little black plastic mouthpiece. Over time, we on the bus have been subjected to her daily tirades, her unceasing catalog of boyfriend complaints. No money, too much money, no sex, too much sex, no alcohol, et cetera. Her mother hated Simon, and after a few months we began to hate Simon too. But now she has met Larry and Larry seems to be an outstanding individual. We on the bus are grateful to Larry and hope, in fact, he marries the chatty say-nothing and takes her home to Toronto or some such place, anywhere the number 147 does not run.

Mother Man is calm. When I first got on this morning, I thought, Oh, dear, he forgot to take his meds today, but he quieted down as soon as we got on the Drive. I call him Mother Man, because these are the words he shouts out suddenly and seemingly uncontrollably from time to time. It's not Tourette's syndrome; I have a nephew with Tourette's. I'm not sure what it is. His head drops down as if he were about to fall asleep, then it jerks straight up, violently, as if he has suddenly been shaken awake from a terrible nightmare. He screams *Mother Man!* sometimes saying it once, sometimes twice. *Mother Man! Mother Man!* I think that's what he's saying. That's what I hear, anyway. It's difficult to tell, when he shouts, if he is frightened or angry. Is it a shout of recognition or a curse?

He is always dressed so carefully, he must live with someone, somebody must be in charge of him. His shirt is usually pressed and goes nicely with whatever pants he has on. The outfits appear to have been put on exactly the way they were laid out for him, the night before, on top of his dresserdrawers. Except for the baseball cap with all the signatures. He never goes without it. It is the one concession his mom or whoever is taking care of him allows, that and the freedom to take the bus on his own. The cap is so beat up and worn, it does not look like anything what a mother would consider "nice," and Mother Man is some mother's son. The signatures are not those of baseball players, however. I know baseball and I didn't recognize a one. Sitting behind him once, I made out the name *Tiger* and concluded he must be a golf enthusiast. Some people are afraid to sit next to him. His eyes are crazy-crossed and his body is lumpen and misshapen. His head is in constant motion, bobbing from left to right, left to right and down, as if he were reading a letter taped to the back of the head of the rider in front of him, a letter written in invisible ink. I have become accustomed to him. And when I hear him scream *Mother Man* these days, it sounds not like a curse to me anymore but something he says to bless himself, to bless us all, something to say out loud so we can all get on with our lovely lives and maybe even make it out to the course with him one day, someday soon.

Finally. The bus starts moving again.

I am excited. A day off with not one single solitary

obligation. Free! The students' plays are read, com-
mented on, and returned, the grades turned in, the
semester over. I don't have to be at work until next year!
Tomorrow morning, I am going home to Florida. I like
traveling on Christmas Day. The airport is deserted and
everyone is on their best behavior, as if there were still a
chance Santa would bring them what they wanted if
only they act right for just one more day. All I have to
do today is go to all the stores where I put things on
hold and pick them up. I had to wait till today to pay
for them; they waited till yesterday to give us our
bonuses at work, the little dickdogs. Of course, for
them a bonus is a bonus, something that supplements,
but for us secretaries a bonus *is* Christmas. Then, afterward, I have an appointment for a manicure with Kim.
How rich-lady is that? First stop, GNC for that paraffin
thing for Mother. They say immersing your hands in
paraffin is good for arthritis, and she suffers terribly
with her hands, those hardworking farm-girl knobs.
Then Studio V for my best friend, Lorraine. I got her an
antique cat mask, a beautiful useless thing for which I
spent the rent but who cares? I know she'll love it and I
love her like I love myself. Cashews from Nuts on Clark
for my motorcycle brother, and the record store for the
CD boxed set of the Rat Pack, his favorite. Then, for
my fashion-plate sister who happens to be one of those
people who knows what to do with a neck scarf, there's

a beautiful silk one at the Art Institute Museum Shop with a picture on it of Renoir's *Two Sisters,* a thing I know she will appreciate because, like her, it is useful, pretty, and appropriate. Then there is the matter of the wrapping paper. This will be my happy stop, my last stop before the manicure. I am often made fun of because when people get a present from me, more often than not the paper is more expensive than the present, but I can't help it. I love paper and this year will be no exception. There is some handmade Japanese paper at The Paper Source with my name all over it. It is royal blue and has a rose-colored edging. If you look carefully, you can see, embedded in the paper, deep down, tiny white baby cranes—princess cranes wading in blue water. Unspeakably lovely. When my brother opens his tin of cashews, though, I must remember to swipe the paper up off the floor before he steps on it with his cowboy boot. He's been taking a lot of long walks in the woods these days, Mother tells me. So. No grocery bags for me today! I am going to wind up at the end of the day with fancy bags from fancy stores just like Pink and Minkie's.

For fun, I have on my fabulous red lamb's-wool coat. It weighs approximately nine hundred pounds, but that's what I like about it. It does the job of keeping you warm, good as down, but at the same time looks pretty. To me, anyway. I got it at my favorite vintage store for forty-five bucks. Forty-five bucks, can you believe it? The only thing it needed was a collar button, which I was thrilled to get, since Buttons and Bows is one of my favorite hangouts. The coat is, I have to admit, a bit much for ten-thirty in the morning. I worried a little when I got on this morning, thinking it might frighten Mother Man, but I managed to pass by his seat unawares. I have spent three stupid winters here looking like the Michelin Tire Man, and enough is enough. One of my office mates saw it and calls it my Pat Nixon coat. But there is absolutely nothing Pat Nixon about it. This is no respectable Republican cloth coat! This is the coat of a naughty libertarian. Independent, at least! To be worn to the opera or to the symphony, by somebody's silky Spanish mistress on their way out of town to who-knows-where. Pat Nixon, my foot. Although I must say I have always had a place in my bleeding liberal heart for her, married to such a nut. I actually met Mrs. Nixon once in Tampa when I was in high school and on the journalism staff. We got out of Geometry to go to a ladies' Republican luncheon fund-raiser, where we were going to interview her for the paper, but we never got the interview. I did get to shake her hand, though, on the way out, and a more courteous and kindly face I have yet to see. I didn't tell her I was not voting for her husband, that I wasn't even old enough yet to vote. But if I had it to live all over again, I would have voted for Richard Nixon most happily. Now that I have lived through a couple of Republican administrations, I have discovered something that comforts my liberal heart when a Republican does win the highest office in the land. Perhaps you, too, have noticed. I find the sex much better under a Republican president. Democrats are the moms and Republicans are the dads! There's something reassuringly illicit about sex when there's a Republican in the White House. You feel deliciously dirty, as if Dad's somewhere in the house, upstairs maybe, and he has no idea you are doing something neither he nor Mr. Green Jeans would entirely approve of. On your grandmother's bedspread with costume jewelry and motor oil, or some such act of insubordination. Sex under Nixon was the best sex this country has ever known, though perhaps I strain the causal connection. Still, it is this thought, and this thought alone, that prevented me from switching my allegiance and moving to Canada recently when what my Texas cousins call the Shrub wormed his way into office.

The next stop is my stop. I gather myself up and stand, in order to begin the long, slow process of making my way to the front. As the bus slows to a halt and I am almost to the door, I see Minkie sitting just to my left. I smile down but she doesn't see me. Isn't this her stop? This is where she and Big Pink always get off. I hesitate to say anything. It's none of my business, of course. She's going someplace different today, that's all. But I look at her. When she's with Pink, they look like two whole people, so now that she is sitting by herself you would think she would look like one. But she doesn't. By herself, she seems less than one. Not even one.

It is noisy in the salon—the busiest day of the year for waxing, pedicures, lash tints—all the preparations a son of God would no doubt expect on the day before the celebration of his birth.

I arrive a little early but Kim is ready for me anyway; her last appointment canceled. She puts my bags in the closet for me, and comes over to her tiny table where I sit. She dunks my one hand in a little blue bath to soak.

What didn't you buy?, she asks, then launches into her latest bingo adventure.

Kim is addicted to bingo. She takes the Milwaukee train every Saturday night to a giant bingo palace there. She says she can make more in one night playing bingo than she makes in a month doing nails. I ask about her son, her daughter, and her mother. They are fucked up, fucked up, and fine, in that order. I catch her up on all my news, which consists of a cute cat story and the trouble I'm having getting a fellow office worker to stop sending me Jesus E-mails.

Florida, huh? That's nice.

I agree that it is indeed nice and find myself suddenly in the unusual position of having absolutely nothing to add. I look down at my hands. I like how your hands feel so clean after a manicure, and I love having no polish. Kim has an electric buffer, and she just makes it so there's a slight shine when she's done. I know all the girls here; I have been coming to this place for centuries. It's a small salon. The owner, Kate, is Polish, and Kim's Korean, but the rest of the beauty makers are originally from Russia. Kim is kind and laughs at all my stupid jokes, but I wouldn't try them out on the Russian girls. These girls have heard it all and seen it all, coming and going: husbands, hairstyles, political regimes. I would not dare say something to them that was not at least Tolstoy, so I wind up not saying anything at all. The most beautiful girl in the salon is Jenny—in Russian, Yevgenya. People don't believe me when I tell them, but her last name is Kiss, her real Russian name, not shortened or anything. Her husband loved her name too, so when they were married, even though it was not a common practice in that time or place, he took *her* name. They gave their children her last name too—pretty wild!—so now there is Jenny Kiss and Chris Kiss and little Mary and Elizabeth Kiss. The Kiss Family Robinson! Or rather, the Russian Family Kiss. It occurs to me, all of a sudden. I'll bet Big Pink and Little Minkie come here.

Florida, huh? You lucky, says Kim.

I smile and say yes and look back down at what Kim's doing and I see something. How many years now—three?—have I been coming here and I never noticed.

There is a scar on Kim's arm a mile long. It starts at the wrist and goes all the way up, past her elbow, after which I can't see because of her sleeve. It's a really big scar.

Kim, I say, pointing.

I've got another one too on my leg, wanna see?

I did not, but she bent down and pulled her white uniform pantleg up and there it was.

What in the world, I said, and she told me,

One time, I was a little girl in Korea, I got burned in a dream.

It is dark when I get on the bus to go home. The faces are dull and grim, carved out of cold and exhaustion and one too many sunshine delays. It is Easter fucking Island in here. Everybody just wants to get the hell home and get the motherfucking Christmas holiday over with. No seats for us tonight, we of the last stop before getting on the Drive. As soon as we realize this, we begin to take the most advantageous positions. I'm tall, so I can hold on to the silver bar way up. The woman beside me is little, so she holds on to the bar at the back of the seat close to her. I put my bags down on the floor, even though it is soggy with melted snow and slush, because I have made sure all my purchases were double-bagged and therefore safe. I place my feet to the left and right of my prized parcels, like bookends. This allows me to hold on with both hands, which minimizes the lurchings, sometimes violent, that can cause you to lose your balance. The temperature has dropped another 30 degrees since this morning, and we've gotten six more inches of snow. It is so cold, you can see your own breath, and we are, please remember, inside. The heater on the bus must be broken, nothing new. People have their parka hoods pulled over their heads and have wound their wool scarves around and around, beginning at the neck and then working all the way up to their eyes, making them look like mean Egyptian mummies. Their eyes do not blink.

It is silent, as if we had all forgotten the language.

A single second goes by. The bus crawls slow as death up Lake Shore Drive. All you can think is, Don't think. Don't *think* anything, don't *say* anything, do not talk, do not say. Conserve each and every granule of energy. If you can hold on a few minutes more, perhaps you may be allowed to live. Perhaps tonight is not the night they mean for you to die. Not here, anyway. Not on a bus, in a modern city. That's just not possible. To die because of weather? Absurd! But we cannot convince even ourselves. It is so cold. In a few minutes, we know we won't be able to feel our toes. We've been through this before, remember? Gosh, it sure would be such a shame to die now, of the cold, in this frozen place, while the rest of the world goes on living. You begin to bargain. At least let me get these lovely presents to their rightful owners so they may enjoy them. It's not their fault I live in this weather-tyrant town. Don't blame the presents! They didn't have a choice. If they'd had a choice, they would have chosen to stay in Tallahassee, a place that's beautiful, a place where people don't die on a bus because somebody in an office forgot to put a stamp on the thing that pays the bill that fixes the thing that doesn't work and causes everybody on the number 147 going north Christmas Eve to die. Nobody's listening, of course, and the bus lumbers slowly along, inch by inch, in what begins to seem not unlike an urban version of the Bataan death march. Just as you think you cannot go on a second longer, you go on a second longer. And then, heaven. The bus stops. You made it! Congratulate yourself! You do not have to die today! You forget instantly, as women after childbirth do, the horrific physical pain to which you were just subjected, and you are so happy you cannot believe your luck, how life could ever be this good. This stop is my stop. *Out, please,* I say, trying not to scream like Mother Man. *I'm getting out, please,* I say, as I make my way up front to the door. I am so happy not to die, so grateful to have been given a second chance, I feel like Jimmy Stewart—I want to live again! I want to live again!—and so I say to the bus driver, as I am getting off, *Merry Christmas, driver!* and take a step down and my bags break.

The bottoms open up like stage trapdoors, giving in to the wetness. The presents spill out, all the beautiful things, all of Christmas, onto the filthy slush and snow, under the bus, onto the pavement, the wind picking up like a mini tornado in the airspace suddenly warmed by the big heaving bus's presence. I am in a cartoon, the antique cat mask, lifted up by the sudden current of air, sails past me as if in a Jim Carrey movie, head high, six feet in the air, out of reach. I am stunned and don't know what to do, so I don't do anything. I've seen people in distress before on the bus, the dropped token, imperative to retrieve because it is the rider's only one and they have to be at work; they're already in trouble. Or the bag of groceries that spills when a mother tries to get on with an infant in one arm and a baby stroller in the other. You see her wretchedness at the sight of a week's worth of suppers going down the drain, but her number one concern is, the look on her face tells you, her shame. She is embarrassed by having caused a scene and in such a public place. Nobody ever helps these people, these people who need help, myself included. We all just sit there and watch and wait and wonder. Whatever will she do now?

And so it is my turn to provide the entertainment.

I step down off the last step and turn around, bend down on my knees to reach under the bus. At first it is hard to see anything because of the darkness. It's only five o'clock at night but it is pitch dark. A little black river has formed in the street right under the bus, and the first thing I make out is the paper. The beautiful blue sheets have fallen free from their bag and are floating away from me in the dark street water. I extend my arm as far from its socket as it can go and actually manage to grab one of the sheets, but as soon as I have it in my hand it begins to dissolve. A wafer-thin bit of pulp is all that remains. I look down into the palm of my hand and see the last princess crane having just lost her first battle with danger.

People are all over me, now, all around. Trampled to death. That is what it will say in tomorrow's headline. TRAMPLED TO DEATH. What better way to go? On my knees, under a bus, in a red forty-five-dollar junk-store coat. How ladylike, how tragic. I can hear Mother, hysterical: *It's all my fault. I'm the one shamed her out of those ugly grocery bags. This never, ever would have happened if I hadn't've scolded her so..* I look up and see. It is not a trampling. People are not trampling me. People are helping me. I am surrounded by people all trying to help me. I am so stunned, I do not comprehend what is happening. One woman double-stuffs her one bag in order to give me her second. *Here, honey. Use this.* Another hands me the cat mask. *I found this in the street. Is it yours?*

Pretty paper, somebody else says. It is Mother Man, and he is holding several of the precious Japanese sheets. I sit up on my knees and take the sheets from him and say thanks. *Thank you,* I say, and see him smile before he walks away. The driver turns in his seat and addresses the rest of the bus. *Listen up, folks. We're not going anywhere. I'm sitting here till this nice lady collects all her things. It's Christmas, people. Let's have a little Christmas spirit here, what do you say?* Everyone is grabbing things and bagging things and removing things from their own bags, asking am I all right, did I hurt myself? Even the Boyfriend Historian tries to help. *Do you want to use my cell phone?*

And then somebody says something quiet, close to my ear.

Don't be embarrassed, dear. It could happen to anyone.

I am still on my knees, but I straighten up. At first I can't see who is speaking to me, it is so very dark, and then I take in the perfume. Chanel Number Five, if I'm not mistaken. It is Little Minkie. She is smiling down at me. I look into her face, grateful—honored, really—to be acknowledged by such a woman. She is all kindness and concern, but there is something else, something untoward. It is a deliberate kindness, a deliberate concern. And now I know. Big Pink is dead.

Merry Christmas, dear, she says to me, and begins to walk away. I stand up as quick as I can to thank her, but she is already at the crosswalk, on her way across the street. I want to say *Merry Christmas to you, too,* but she is already out of sight, already dissolved back into the black and the cold, and as I go back down on my knees, continuing to retrieve what can be retrieved, I see the street water, laced with city salt, has drained the color from the skirt of my coat. The red has bled completely out, and for the first time I begin to see how easy it is, how quick it can happen. For the world to take a turn for the pink.

Once, in Hamburg

Once, in Hamburg, Daralynn prevented us from getting kidnapped and worse by three giant Turks. Lucky for us we had the peanut butter. The peanut butter was one thing Daralynn carried in her purse when we went on trips together: that, the passports, and the cash. I was in charge of the hand lotion and the matchbook sewing kit. This is the kind of arrangement that is worked out by girlfriends all over the world, and Daralynn and I had been friends since ninth grade, since the day she'd walked into homeroom eating a raw onion as if it were an apple. I worshiped her.

And it is that onion that divides humanity. The onion explains what happened in Hamburg that day in the back of that Chevrolet with those three gigantic Turks. It is the onion that divides the Daralynns of the world from my kind. My kind stands paralyzed in the face of adversity, like a toad in front of a coiled viper. In dreams, we are blonde stalks of wheat standing tall before the combine, waiting our turn in perfectly parallel rows, knowing, as a stalk of wheat would know, the jig is up.

She had this purse. It was like a box, it could stand up on its own. It had big red splotches all over it that I said looked just like cherry suckers, like the ones we used to get at McCrory's. Daralynn said they were ancient Tibetan mandalas. It closed at the top with a leather drawstring.

She said she got it out of a catalog from New York that her cousin sent her; it was made by real monks in Katmandu, and the leather was cured in their very own urine, which was one reason it took six months to get to Brunswick—that's Georgia—which is where we're from. To me it looked more like something her Uncle Buck fashioned out of an old hide on her graduation day, thinking to himself, This is just the ticket.

Besides the peanut butter, Daralynn carried a bottle of Windex in her purse. What's the point of Europe, she said, if you can't see it? It made me uneasy, knowing that our only food source and a household cleanser made with Ammonia-D were commingling at the bottom of a leather bag soaked in monk pee. Daralynn said I was anal; it only went to show my Virgo rising, and I should read Susan Sontag on the self-contained before I turned twenty-one—the age, she said, at which the brain's supply of sodium and potassium begins to diminish.

She wore the purse like a street fighter, slung over one shoulder. We were nineteen. We had done California. We had done Colorado. Now we were going to do Europe.

We went first to London. Everything confirmed our suspicion that America was somewhere to be ashamed of. Betty Crocker, Borden's, Kraft bruised our ears, and our allegiance turned, by some twist of faith, to the new names. Chambourcy, McVities, Typhoo. We were college sophomores in London, thrilled to be college sophomores in London, thrilled to have an address on Cromwell Road. We began to use the word "remarkable."

"Look at that," Daralynn said, pointing to the cover of *Time Out*. "Jim Morrison ejaculated on stage in Miami."

"That's remarkable," I said. "What's *ejaculate?*"

The way she explained it, I pictured this giant salt shaker being held upside down, pouring forth, floored why anybody'd want to pee onstage in front of people. I imagined had Daralyn been there, she would have collected the stuff and sent it off to Katmandu, where it could be used for the making of ladies' handbags.

We'd been in London for less than a week when Daralynn announced we were going to Istanbul.

"Istanbul?" I said. "Why can't we just go see the Eiffel Tower like everybody else?"

"Because," said Daralynn.

"Because why? What's wrong with the Eiffel Tower?"

"Look. Renan gave me her parents' number."

"We're going to stay with the hotel maid?"

"With her parents."

"Who we've never in our lives even met?"

"Who we've never in our lives even met."

"What about Rome? What about going to the Colosseum and getting the fever like we planned?"

"We can stay free," Daralynn pointed out. "Her parents own a summerhouse right on the Sea of Marmara."

"But the Fountain of Travail. What about going to pick up Dutch boys at the Fountain of Travail?"

"Plus," said Daralynn, "Renan's mother is famous. She sings opera."

"*Is* an opera singer," I said.

"That's what I said," Daralynn said.

"You can't *sing* opera. You can sing country, you can sing rock 'n' roll, but you can't *sing* opera."

It was a great moment for me. Daralynn had always gotten away with everything. Her powers of persuasion were such that she was able in our senior year in high school to get her whole family to go on a brown rice diet, even her dad, a career serviceman, a man not unaccustomed to using the word *prioritize* at breakfast. My parents voted for McGovern and I couldn't get them to let me stay out past ten o'clock at night with a Methodist.

We went.

You know that *Twilight Zone* episode, the one where

the string-mop head teenager lives as an outcast on a planet full of humanoids, and the regular humanoid kid lives on a planet full of string-mops? In Turkey, I was blonde and tall, where everybody else is dark and small. I was a girl in Istanbul, where everybody else is a man.

We took a *dolmisch* to the parents' house. They greeted us at the door, dark little twins.

"Hello," we said.

"Hello," they said.

Daralynn and I understood immediately we were sluts. The father took our bags and disappeared down a dark corridor.

Truth was, Daralynn at least qualified, while I—to my own dismay—didn't come close. Back home, the best of my conquests was a ride home from school with a violinist, first chair. While Daralynn, and this by her second quarter freshman year, had smoked dope with the son of a Republican senator, downed shots backstage in Atlanta with B. B. King, slept in a boxcar with a member of the Cherokee Nation, and seduced at the Holiday Inn Downtown, right next to where her father takes his Pontiac for repairs, our Religion 101 teacher, a full professor, one of the few people you meet in a lifetime who can use "inasmuch as" in almost every sentence and get away with it. "Inasmuch as" Buber this. "Inasmuch as" Tillich that. He had known Albert Schweitzer intimately.

Renan's mother showed us into the living room and asked would we like coffee.

"Yes," we said. "That would be great. We love coffee." Thinking this might not be enough, I added, "We drink it all the time at home."

Renan's father came into the living room and motioned for us to take a seat on the couch. As soon as I saw that couch I knew I was had. The cushions were the kind, when you sit on them, you sink way way down, and I knew the instant I sat down, my skirt would ride up, way up, beyond the slut line, so I offered to help with the coffee. I beamed like the village idiot and walked out of the room, heading for the kitchen, not needing directions, led by the smell of something foul. I was almost there and glad of it when I heard Daralynn say to the father, "I am very concerned about Renan's teeth."

Daralynn had this thing about teeth. She was horrified the day I confessed to having a crush on that guy in *Belle de Jour,* the one who plays Catherine Deneuve's lover. He has two silver front teeth, the rest are all crooked and sawed off, really erotic. Daralynn, of course, has perfect teeth. All her cousins are dentists. She was shocked when we arrived at Heathrow. The British have the worst teeth. "All those scones and then to only have the National Health."

"Hello," I said to the mother. "Can I help?"

Renan's mother said nothing. I spotted a jar of Nescafé

on the counter, and the sight of the familiar logo comforted me, so I said, "What a nice kitchen you have."

She did not say, The better to feed you with, my dear.
She asked if I spoke French at all, her English was not so
very good.

"*Un petit,*" I said shyly, looking at the floor.

"*Bon,*" she said.

There was a big black pan warming on the stove. She
went over to one set of cupboards and took down a silver
tray. She went over to the other set of cupboards and took
down four little cups and four little saucers to match,
placing them carefully on the silver tray. Then she took
the jar of Nescafé and measured out two teaspoons into
each cup. She walked over to the stove and took the big
black pan from off the burner. She went over to the
cups, pan in hand, turned, looked me straight in the
eye, and began to pour. I watched in horror as big lumps
of skin landed like dumplings in each cup. Homoge-
nized, it wasn't.

"Mmm," I said.

"*Bon,*" she said.

The third cup from the left had the fewest number of
lumps in it, so I followed it back out into the living room,
where Daralynn was holding forth. It was her Artistic Vision
Is Not All That Mysterious conversation, her personal best.

"Artistic vision," she was saying, "is not all that
mysterious."

The father was holding on to every word. Being concerned about Renan's teeth had paid off. The father, who was seated in the father's chair, looked straight at my hemline, scowled, and turned back to Daralynn.

"Take the invention of tubes, for example. Look at Van Gogh."

I sat down in the wooden rocker, realizing too late. This was the mother's chair.

"What a nice day," I said. "Is it always this nice?"

The mother took the only seat left, the baby chair, and stared straight into the air in front of me.

"*Il fait beau, n'est-ce pas?*" I said.

She rested her gaze just above my brow line. She seemed to notice something, something far away in the distance, something familiar, a crucifixion, perhaps.

"What Van Gogh did," Daralynn was saying, "he squeezed paint straight out of the tube, like toothpaste."

"In Georgia," I said, "where we're from, it's usually so sticky this time of year." I asked the mother if she thought it would be as nice tomorrow as it had been today.

"*Bon,*" she said.

"Like I'm saying," Daralynn was saying, "before tubes, Van Gogh could never've been Van Gogh. It's technology—that's what art historians are unwilling to admit. Technology has played a large part in allowing the artist to arrive to his particular vision."

"*At* his particular vision," I said.

The mother leaned over and gave Daralynn the third cup from the left.

As the afternoon fell, the foul odor coming from the kitchen became more pronounced. Renan's mother asked what we'd like to drink with dinner, and I said, "Nothing, thank you." Daralynn said Coke and got it.

"Don't you want to ask for a skirt to go with that?" I teased.

Daralynn gave me a terrible look, warning me not to explain.

Now I love Daralynn with all my heart, as only a best friend can. I'd step in front of a truck for her. But being best friends with somebody affords you certain rights. And I felt it well within my rights at that moment to point out to her that she had, by shushing me up just then, abrogated a certain loyalty, the kind of loyalty prohibiting the shushing up of one's best friend in front of people, particularly in front of people you know do not like you. Had someone else tried to point this out to her, I would have beaten them bloody. But as her best friend it was my duty.

Before I got the chance, however, we were called to dinner. The father indicated to Daralynn that she was to sit at his right hand. I took the place across from her. In the center of the table, there was a beautiful plastic place mat with a picture of the Eiffel Tower on it. Out came the mother, smiling, carrying a big silver tray with a big silver cover.

Lamb's eyes, I thought. Fish juice. Flies with vinegar. She set the covered dish on the Eiffel Tower. She smiled. The father smiled. Daralynn, then me. Up stood the father and across the table he leaned. Off came the lid. I almost forgave Daralynn everything as soon as I saw. It was fried chicken.

All through dinner, nobody could get enough of Daralynn. The mother spoke perfect English to her and begged to be allowed to fix her hair after dinner, never had she seen such lovely hair. She even tossed me a smile or two. The father unwrapped a little cake of halvah for dessert, and having dessert made me feel more at home. I told the father how much I liked halvah, how delicious dinner had been, and what a nice country Turkey was, but he gave the biggest piece to Daralynn. After dinner we watched *The Fugitive* on TV.

After five days, Daralynn decided we should be moving along. At the airport, Daralynn promised the father she'd make sure Renan got to a dentist first thing, she'd see to it personally. We promised to write every day and recited our addresses, but the mother didn't begin writing until Daralynn gave hers.

"Goodbye," they said.

"Goodbye," we said, and boarded our flight to Luxembourg.

Our plan was to fly to Luxembourg and take the train to Paris. Daralynn had made that compromise, but when we landed in Luxembourg she announced that we were going to Bergen.

"Norway? Why Norway?"

"*Everybody* goes to Paris," were her first and last words on the subject. She had the passports. She had the cash. "Hamburg, Copenhagen, a ferry to Oslo, the train to Bergen. We can get back to London by ship. Bergen to Newcastle." She'd had it planned from the start.

But when we got to Hamburg, Daralynn discovered her wallet was missing. We hadn't gotten traveler's checks because Daralynn said traveler's checks were bourgeois. I had a little change, but after breakfast we were broke.

"But not penniless," I put in, giving her every ounce of Doris Day I could muster. "I've still got my pennies."

Don't ask me, but when we were packing to leave America, I emptied out all the pennies from my clown penny bank into a tiny velvet pouch that zippered shut. I kept it in my purse, sandwiched between the hand lotion and the matchbook sewing kit. I was beginning to long for amber waves of grain at this point, and the familiar sight of the little copper Lincolns somehow comforted me. Daralynn said we'd have to hitchhike to Amsterdam, then wire home for money. I said, Why don't we just wire home from here? but she said it would be an experience.

"Hitchhiking is perfectly safe if you know how to do it," she said. She'd read the State Department's brochure.

We found our way to the highway. Two cars pulled over. One was a gray Jaguar, the kind of gray that's so subtle it leaves you wondering whether it's really gray or not. A rich lady in a fur coat was driving it. The other car was a green Chevrolet low-rider, rusted out of its mind. There were three guys in it. I headed for the Jag, but Daralynn took my arm and steered me toward the low-rider saying, Get smart; life's a paradox; you should know that by now.

Daralynn prided herself on being a terrific judge of human character. Appearances can be deceiving, she'd say to me, that's the lesson of *Othello*. But there had been times she'd been wrong. Mr. Fairweather, for instance, our high school English teacher. She thought he'd asked her to come by his office after school because he wanted to talk about how interesting her poetry was. As Daralynn explained it to me later, he seemed instead to be going through a certain stage in his development that encouraged him to be demonstrative about his maleness.

There were three guys in the car. One got out of the front seat and opened the back door for us. I slid in first, smiling at what was inside. Daralynn got in after me, then the other guy. We were the cheese. As the click of the locks sounded, first on my side, then on Daralynn's, my brain clicked into its This Is Not Happening mode. I watched as the gray Jaguar sped off down the highway and I thought, this is the part of the story where two hippie chicks from Brunswick, Georgia, get raped and quartered in the backseat of a Chevrolet just outside of Hamburg by three gigantic Turks. It would be *our* story on the cover of the next edition of the State Department's brochure. The headline would read ONCE, IN HAMBURG, and there'd be an interview with the lady in the Jaguar. She'd be saying, "They seemed like such *nice* girls."

Daralynn was excited. She was talking a mile a minute to the guy on her side. She'd just found out they were Turkish. "What karma!" she said. "We just got back from there." She asked where, in Turkey, were they from.

I looked at the guy next to me. He was poking the index finger of his right hand in and out of a fist he'd made with his left hand. This I took to be an international sign. I turned to Daralynn, but she wasn't paying attention. She was telling the driver how we wanted to go in the direction of Bremen and did he happened to know the fairy tale about the Three Mules of Bremen; oh, he must; fairy tales have a universal significance. But when she saw the sign to Bremen pointing this way and saw our driver going that way, even Daralynn quieted down. We turned onto an unpaved road.

We were out of the city now. There were a few farm-houses, but it was mostly fields. My guy said something to her guy that tickled the driver pink. He looked into the rearview—his eyebrows thick like mean black anthills—and said something that sounded like "giggle bears," looking at me. I started to tear up but Daralynn pinched me hard.

It was sunny. Not a cloud in the sky. Daralynn had on my favorite skirt. I was always borrowing it to go to Bergman movies, which is where I thought I was going to meet HIM. It was white and wrinkled; Daralynn's mother was forever trying to iron it. It fell down evenly in three equidistant tiers, which I said made it look like a wedding cake and which Daralynn said was structurally identical to a Babylonian ziggurat.

The skirt fell down over Daralynn's purse, wedged between her feet on the floor. She said something to me in French I didn't understand and then bent over and reached deep into her purse and pulled out the jar of peanut butter. Her guy looked interested. Cows appeared, now, on either side of the road. They too looked interested.

It was a brand-new jar, so it took her some effort to get it open. My guy offered to help but Daralynn said no, thanks, she had it.

She placed the lid carefully on her guy's knee. Using her hand as a spade, she scooped out a handful of peanut butter and began to apply it to her face like cold cream.

Then down her blouse. She turned to her guy—I didn't see this part; she told me later—and, smiling like a geisha, she drooled.

Her guy hissed, then yelled to the driver. The car swung over to the side of the road. The locks unclicked, her guy jumped out, and we were shoved and kicked and thrown to the ground. Doors slammed. There was dirt in the air. We looked up. The car spun around in the dirt, caught, and hesitated for a moment. My guy rolled down his window and spit. The car took off.

It took the rest of the day to get back to town. Daralynn didn't say a word. She seemed tired way out of proportion. It was windy that day. I noticed Daralynn's skirt kept riding up, making it hard for her to walk. But instead of being irritated by this, she acted embarrassed. Her slip was showing.

We came to a little park, and Daralynn asked could we sit down for a minute and I said sure, pleased with my new role as travel consultant. It was then that we noticed. Bells were ringing. And had been ringing the whole time we'd been in Hamburg, but we hadn't actually heard them until we sat down. We were sitting on a little bridge that went over a little pond where there were ducks and swans and geese all swimming. The wind was blowing like crazy and the bells kept ringing. They were ringing so hard, we decided the king must be dead. It must be something that big. It surprised me that Daralynn did not point out the political naïveté of this remark but in fact kept insisting, over and over, to no one in particular, Yes, that's it, the king must be dead. We sat for a long time in silence.

"Give me your hem," I said.

"What?"

"Your hem, Miss Priss." I took out my matchbook sewing kit. "I'm going to sew pennies into your hem."

"What for?"

"To keep your skirt from riding up."

I remember her hair. It kept getting tangled up in my needle. When it got tangled up in my needle, she would get this look on her face. She would look at me as if she had something to say, retrieve the maverick strands, and allow me to go on with my stitching. But her hair would get tangled up in my needle again. The wind was crazy that day, and she would get that look again. She would get that look again, like a schoolgirl, take back the rebel strands, and let me go on with my stitching.

It occurred to me at this moment that Daralynn was a great beauty. I had never thought about her that way before, but I looked at her and saw, and I was filled with pride that my best friend was so beautiful.

And I thought to myself, If I didn't have Daralynn, I might have gone through my whole life as the string-mop kid. I might have gone through my whole life not knowing what *ejaculate* was, how terrific a process homogenization was. I might never have gone to Istanbul, might never have done anything remarkable at all, like sew pennies into the skirt of a great beauty, in Hamburg, in the wind, with the bells ringing, the day the king died.

"Wake up," said Daralynn, "or they're going to come put pennies over your eyes."

"That's from your Uncle Buck," I said.

"That's from my Uncle Buck."

The reason I kidded Daralynn about wanting a skirt to go with her Coke was because of her Uncle Buck. Daralynn's Uncle Buck drank a Coke at ten-thirty every morning no matter what, one of those perfect six-ounce Cokes with the city where it came from on the bottom.

He had sewn elastic around one side of a pink potholder—he didn't like his hand to get wet—and on summer mornings, no matter where you stood on his squat shoestring farm, you'd know on any given day when it was ten-thirty because you could hear him call, "Daralynn, run go get me my Co-Cola with a skirt." He'd always make us guess which city, and Daralynn would say things like Katmandu or Istanbul. But I wasn't ashamed of her Uncle Buck, so I guessed Mobile. Tuscaloosa. Yellow River City.

Redlight

There's something about academe that, every once in a while, with no forewarning, brings out the Charles Bronson in me, locked somewhere way way down in the Pabst-strewn garage apartment of my soul. I don't know whether it's when my bookish compatriots, deep in complaint, announce, "This jerk doesn't know the difference between a dependent clause and his own big fat foot"; whether it's the hospital green that follows me along the quiet corridor, making students patients, making me the sometime doctor, a blonde quack; or whether it's my own snobbish inclination to tell a student who said he just read *A Grape of Wrath* that perhaps he should pursue a career in dentistry. Don't get me wrong. I think there's a lot of sex in book chat. But that sort of response seems harder and harder to call up, let alone generate. Nobody "just loves" *anybody* anymore. The

Romantics were too silly, the Realists too bloodless, Shake-speare too well known, and Beckett—well, even he never really wanted to talk about it. You can't leave a love note in a Keats collection in the stacks anymore and be assured of a phone call. There are no stacks. Nobody runs up to you in the hall and tells you, "You gotta read this, you gotta read this!" Instead, it's "So-and-so's talk" on post-something or other was "well put, insightful." Your students' papers are "well put, insightful." Even the juiciest of departmental gossip is "well put, insightful." It's why I drive stiff through traffic lights that have been amber for a block. A third-grade response, granted, but it's one way I have of registering desire.

So that over Christmas break, when after just enough cocaine but too much tequila I woke up next to a total stranger, next to Danny Hawk—Danny Hawk who has a tattoo of a hawk on his left arm, Danny Hawk who has an arm the width of my head, Danny Hawk who rode in from Austin on a Harley to play bass for "some fellas" at a down-and-out where knifings and waitresses leave sadder and wiser men, Danny Hawk who is not at all my body type—it was as if Jesus (or whoever's doing all this) had sent me a per-sonalized heaven-stamped present, gift-wrapped in leather, sealed with a beery kiss. I've slept with an elevator operator, a violinist, one grocer, two felons, a molecular biophysicist, three guitarists (acoustic), and a typewriter repairman, but never, never ever, a man with—well, musculature.

When I saw the tattoo, I had to pinch myself. Is this me? Is this the same person who earlier in the week scolded Cindy Davis for not skipping lines on her in-class essay on "The Love Song of J. Alfred Prufrock"? Is this the same person who downgraded Ronny Watson for mistaking *paranoia* for *feeling insignificant* in body paragraph three? Who lowered Karen Connolly's paper half a letter grade for not counting her words? Who scalded them all for not paginating their journals? Who raves, week in and week out, to Chrissie and Jimmy and Stacie and Tracy never again to begin an introduction with the words "In today's modern American society, there are many various different kinds of people." When he woke up, I had to ask him if we did it.

I own this not-so-bad reproduction of a Goltzius engraving, *Henry IV, King of France*. Late sixteenth century. It was my first real purchase as an adult, the first thing I didn't get at a flea market or steal or have given me. Goltzius was this Dutch virtuoso engraver who had a kind of absolute bloodless skill only a Virgo can enjoy, like he was doing it on graph paper, but of course he wasn't. He used to have fun fooling connoisseurs by duplicating Parmigianino and Lucas van Leyden and big guys like that. Anyway, when I came out of the shower, Danny Hawk says, "Guy looks like a real drag," leaning Neanderthal into this my prize engraving, and I say, "Do you really think so?" and he says yeah so I say, "I mean, how can you tell?" and he says, "You can tell," so I say, "I think you're right about that," and he says yeah and I say, "Yeah, I think you've got something there." He walks with enormous disinterest across the room and drops into my gooseneck rocker, knocking my cat Betty off, causing her to land without grace, a position she's unaccustomed to, and puts his muddied boot up on my teak table, right on the pansy doily made by nuns underwater that my mom got in Brussels on her honeymoon in 1947. I think I'm in love with this guy. At least he doesn't stand in front of the kitchen cabinet every morning wondering whether to have Earl Grey or Lapsang Soochong, which is my daily dilemma. So I try to put my sweater on violently this time, just to impress him, wrenching the sleeves up purposefully, instead of my usual insecure swipe at the cuffs. He seems to notice I'm ready (we're on our way to breakfast) and lifts his jacket off the couch to go. Everything that says yes inside me hoped for a reptile on the back, so my heart sank when I saw the black swan. It wasn't the first time I'd been disappointed by a swan.

When I was ten and we lived in France, my mother, who was into holistic healing and the laying on of hands and other stuff I didn't know was weird until later, thought she'd take me, her forever ill and pale child, to Vittel, to the healing waters of Vittel. I was scared. I never saw so many crippled people in one place before. The water looked like they'd all peed in it and smelled worse than my brother's shoe closet and the formaldehyde at the school science lab put together. My mother gave me one of those well-if-you-want-to-be-an-invalid-all-your-life looks, so I held my breath and went in for love. I thought about Saint Teresa and how she ate her patients' excrement, which was the only thing I could think of at the time that could be worse. On the way home we stopped at a lovely little park and ate *jambon* and drank *limonade* by a lovely little pond where some swans were, which was more what I had in mind in the first place. I was a big fan of the Ugly Duckling story and awaited the transformation daily. Well, the story was right. The swans were beautiful—graceful, balletic, their timing perfect, as if they ran on batteries. But when I went to the edge of the pond for a closer inspection, I saw, just beneath the water's surface, the biggest ugliest orange flappers you'd ever want to see, madly paddling beneath, trying, it seemed to me at the time a little desperately, to live up to their reputation. It was my first really significant disappointment.

I followed Danny Hawk's swan out the front door and got on the back of his Harley as if I'd done it before. This was no time to play dumb. This guy was the real thing. He was what the Crystals were singing about in, "He's a Rebel." Not quite Charles Bronson but rough nonetheless. I made him stop at my drive-up bank, unsure if he were accustomed to paying for his food. I don't know about you, but I was a sophomore in college before I found out what banks do with money. I'd imagined the safe to be like one of those old gentlemen's clothing stores, a room full of old cedar drawers with everybody's name in script, and there'd be one drawer with my name on it—my social security number, to be sure but nonetheless my name, in prestige elite typeface, no doubt, but my name nevertheless. And the dough inside in one-dollar bills. Richer people had bigger drawers. Then at the end of the month some Bartleby-like guy a hundred years old would count it all up—enter it on some computer-processor thingamajig, surely, but count it (tabulate it digitally)—finger it nevertheless. And register the sum to the authorities. When the digital explanation was given me, it was probably my second most significant disappointment.

We exit the bank and head for Sambo's. He takes a corner too fast. "Like that?" he yells. I want him. Now. Up on the curb. Now, in this guy's half-mown lawn with the little ceramic bird feeder. Asphalt bedding and our jackets zipped all the way up. At our house, *adultery* was thought, in the most catholic sense of the word, to include anything you did without intent of marriage. Our coffee-table Bible was always opened to this picture of heaven, with Jesus in a dress, and hair like he'd just gotten a Toni, and a lot of little boys without scars or hearing impairments sitting at his feet. I loved Jesus with all my heart then, as only a ten-year-old girl can, and my daydreams about going to heaven to live with him started out with this scene and him welcoming me and all (my slate clean, since I'd never done any of that stuff—steal, kill, covet—the ten things we were politely reminded not to do on a bookmark that accompanied this picture of Jesus, a chain of gold-penny-like links). But the scene would change and there I'd be on the set of *To Tell the Truth* with impostors on either side of me and Garry Moore reading my affidavit. In a moment I would have to walk down and face Tom Poston, Peggy Cass, Bill Cullen, and Kitty Carlisle, knowing, as all impostors know, the jig was up.

At Sambo's, Danny Hawk acts regular. So I say, "Why don't I fix supper for just the two of us tonight while you're setting up equipment?" and he says sure, fine, with enormous disinterest. When he asks the waitress for Tabasco for his fried eggs, I swoon. I think, When I get home, I won't tidy up. I'll stick all my Mel Tormé albums in the back of the stack and put Janis Joplin up front. Early Hendrix, early Stones. I will not make him *crema di pomodori,* a Florentine dish; it has cream in it. I will not put on soft underthings. This was a no-underthing kind of guy. I will not serve wine in my Sorrento crystal but in coffee mugs, beige and office-ugly. I'll make something with hamburger in it. I wish I had the Veg-E-Matic I worried my mother to death over before she finally sent away for it. I thought at the time it would make me popular with Steve Scurlock, who loved french fries. Only when it came, the blades weren't sharp enough to dice a mushroom. You had to sit on it to get the potato to go all the way down.

Out of Sambo's, on the ride home with Danny Hawk, I slide in closer and reposition my hold—something schoolmarm types have been getting away with unde-tected for centuries. We approach the biggest intersection in town. The light's yellow and we're a block away. I lean, Neanderthal as I can get, into his big black swan. I want to risk it: the Veg-E-Matic, the baths at Vittel, the bank account, everything. Risk the whole lame, watered-down thing. We both know it's going to turn red, as I think, How'm I ever gonna get this one past Peggy Cass—she's so smart—and I think maybe that guy who read *A Grape of Wrath* really liked it, really enjoyed it, maybe even ran down the corridor, hospital green, of his dorm and told this other guy, Rob: Hey, Rob, you gotta read this, you gotta read this! Danny Hawk smiles in the rearview as I go, for the first time not stiff, past the intersection, past the redlight, past disappointment.

I will make him such french fries.

A History of the Pandas

Part One: Bright and Shiny

I am sitting at my kitchen table waiting for the restaurant to come back on the phone. My sister will be here any minute. She's taking a cab from the airport. At least the house is ready.

Lydia's visit is something of a mystery. She called to say she was coming to Chicago for a one-day seminar, childhood something-or-other. If it was okay by me, she'd fly in the night before, I could pick the restaurant, her treat. It was the "her treat" part that made me think something must be up. That made it an overture. I've lived in Chicago for ten years and she's never wanted to visit before. We see each other twice a year, in Florida at mother's for Christmas or Thanksgiving and then at the timeshare in August. We talk on the phone all the time, mostly recipe chat. TRY IT WITH PEARS. She said this to me quietly the other day after I had been bragging non-stop about the garlic-studded lemons I placed inside my roast chicken, a dish I have been presenting for centuries to the global applause of ex-boyfriends everywhere. Pears with garlic? TRY IT WITH PEARS. I tried it with pears. Un-be-fuck-a-lievable. Wisely, when Mother downsized the house after our father died, she gave Lydia the recipes. I got the family bowling ball.

This has got to be one of the dumber centuries. I'm only calling to confirm. I made the reservation weeks ago. Charlemagne wouldn't have this problem.

No, I answer myself, he wouldn't. There weren't any restaurants in Charlemagne's time. Seven hundred years after is when restaurants came to be. After all the mams and messieurs got their heads lopped off so their cooks found themselves out of a job and *voilà!*

Nothing I know does me any good.

In honor of my sister's visit I have dug out the old Doris Day album *Bright and Shiny.* We were raised on this thing. I inherited the family record collection. My sister got the button box. I turn the ancient album cover over and notice something for the first time. Pointless optimism, I see, with a measured amount of horror, was not the only thing my sister and I learned from Doris Day.

On the back of the album are three photographs of Doris

dressed in three different outfits. In the first, Miss Day is a long black exclamation mark. Black turtleneck descends to black stretch pants, which descend to black patent-leather flats. Her hands rest coy on her hips in emphatic black cotton gloves. Think Catwoman on her way to church.

In the second photograph, the idea of science is introduced. Doris stands in front of living room drapes upon which swinging rectangles, jolly rhombuses, and bouncing parallelograms sway to a glad-handing beat. Cool Daddi-O. An isosceles triangle of a car coat teeters on her shoulders like a cockeyed lampshade, though she is fully fulcrumed to the floor via a cheerful symmetry of heels, gloves, earrings, and hair. The hair, impossibly blonde, is an ear-length flip, one on each side, which on anyone else would announce a British court magistrate of an earlier century but on Miss Day reveals the fun of science, of all good things that make perfect sense. What you see here is the geometry of happiness.

I make money talking about Kafka. I teach Intro-to-Lit classes to art students at an art college where our school colors are black and black. My clothes say Go away. Go as physically far away from me as you personally can, in this elevator, on this plane, this planet. I have eaten things you would not step on. Now, after lo these many years, to come to find out my role model of fashion has all along been Doris Day—Doris Day as Catwoman but still Doris Day—well, it's disturbing.

My sister's clothes say Give me a hug. She is Doris number two. She teaches at a preschool in Los Angeles where everything really is bright and shiny. Children swarm around her like pink happy planets. Come sit on my lap, her clothes say. Parents come to pick their children up in the afternoon. They sit on her lap too, and I don't blame them. My sister has always been an entirely persuasive individual. She could talk Socrates into leading an unexamined life. I see him seated at her kitchen table, shaking his head, saying to himself, What was I thinking? as he reaches for another of my sister's Toll House dreams.

There is another side to her, though, not even Socrates can see.

In the third photograph, Doris is a blizzard in white. Think tundra. As in frozen completely solid.

YOU'RE SCARING THE KITTENS.

Ricky thinks I've gone overboard. I have cleaned this apartment within an inch of its life and it knows it—the sheets ironed and lavendered, the spices alphabetized. Compared to me, Martha Stewart is a ten-dollar crack whore passed out on a cold kitchen floor strewn with dirty, if cleverly crocheted, syringes. Last night, as I made the inspection tour, room by room, the furniture cowered in fear.

Ricky's idea of having company over is to open a bag

of Bugles and set it on the coffee table, equidistant between my *National Geographic*s and his six-pack of nothing much. For special, he will roll down the top several inches of the bag. It makes a lovely silver cuff.

He got me the kittens for my birthday, three little white cotton puffballs. He put them in a shoebox he had poked holes into. I turned forty-two Saturday, and he's twenty-seven. I know it's bad, but guys my age are so old, and I don't mind explaining who John Prine is.

IT'S NOT LIKE THE QUEEN OF ENGLAND OR SOMETHING. SWEETHEART, SHE'S YOUR SISTER. SHE'S ONLY GOING TO BE HERE ONE NIGHT.

I try to explain how it *is* like the Queen of England or something, but I don't quite understand it myself.

I JUST WANT THINGS TO BE NICE.

EVERYTHING IS NICE, PUMPKIN.

I WANT HER TO LIKE MY CHAIRS.

YOUR SISTER IS GOING TO FLIP WHEN SHE SEES YOUR CHAIRS. NOW COME ON OR WE'LL MISS THE PREVIEWS.

Ricky's real name is Richard. He lets me call him Ricky and I let him call me pumpkin. He likes me because I fill in the art portion of the program and I have blonde hair. I like him because he listens all the way to the end of my sentences. He doesn't just wait till I'm done and then start in, trumping my information with his information. He considers what I say, so in return I try not to say everything I know. He has the sweetest internal darkroom where he lets things sit and develop. Like last night after the movie when I told him John Goodman was the cyclops. Ricky doesn't read what I read, so he thought what I said was interesting. We had supper at our favorite place. Ricky had his number 32 and I had my *muc sate,* and then we went to his place for entirely blameless sex. This morning, the first thing he says to me, we're in bed:

SO THE GIRLS IN SLIPS, THE GIRLS DOWN BY THE RIVER, WASHING?

We said it together, then dissolved back sweet into each other.

Sirens.

He thinks we should move in together, but I know better.

THOSE KITTENS DON'T COUNT AS A COMMITMENT? he argued.

BANGS, I told him. BANGS ARE A COMMITMENT.

If there's one thing I've learned in forty-two years of failed romance, it's that relationship chat is a killer.

Ricky doesn't mind my rough talk. You can't insult him because he's comfortable in what he knows. He's a veterinarian. What he knows helps the animals. Before Ricky, it was a long line of the overeducated and underwhelmed— the last one so *Lingua Franca* like you wouldn't believe. He used to beat me up with his information on a nightly basis. Ricky just found out there's a *p* in raspberry and he was fucking delighted! *Live and learn,* was his only comment. Literature, in my humble opinion, and its accompanying body of knowledge, is unable to help with the animals—or anyone else for that matter. But Ricky's right. I have gone overboard. When I walk into the living room, the kittens line up alphabetically—Betty, Eddie, and Nixon. They stand at attention, willing one another not to shed. Perhaps I clean for my sister because it's something I *can* do. Other things, not so much. Like perform a resurrection.

I THOUGHT HER HUSBAND, ALL THAT, WAS ANCIENT HISTORY, PUMPKIN. I MEAN, IT'S TRAGIC, OF COURSE.

YOU'RE ANCIENT HISTORY. NOW KISS ME AND GET LOST.

Ricky's gone to Seattle for three days to give a talk on feline leukemia. Twenty years ago, I suppose, is ancient history, from the standpoint of a cat.

I just recently learned how to poach an egg without its feathering all to hell in the pan so I can appreciate a fine dining experience as much as the next person, but jeezus penis, who do these people think they are? The universe hears my bad thought and my reservation is confirmed: two for eight. I hang up the phone. The cordless world has thus far eluded me.

Did you know there are one thousand one hundred and seventy-nine restaurants in the Chicagoland area? After a few onsite visits and calling everyone I have ever met, I had it boiled down to two. But the French place turned out to be too French, and the Italian not Italian enough. Ricky suggested I take her to the Tiki Palace. He loves the piña colada pork plate they serve there. I just looked at him. Besides the fact that it is a shit hole, it puts pineapple in everything, and for my sister pineapple is a problem.

Soon after her husband was murdered, my sister Lydia developed an allergic reaction to pineapple. This was unfortunate since one of her favorite dishes, an old family recipe, was a lime Jell-O mold consisting of lime Jell-O, cottage cheese, the now-verboten pineapple, pecans, and a genius teaspoon of horseradish, a concoction we knew growing up as Daddy Bob's Delite, spelled "l-i-t-e" not so much as a reflection of any low caloric intake as it was of the general family optimism, an optimism rigorously enforced. Our house ran on three records. Mahalia Jackson for after church, Mel Tormé for after supper, and Doris Day, "Bright and Shiny," for everything in between. My mother's favorite was the Doris Day. The songs on this album emphasized the importance of maintaining, come what may, both a clean household and a sunny disposition: "Bright and Shiny," "Twinkle and Shine," "Be Happy," "Make Someone Happy," "Forget Your Troubles and Just Get Happy." In the event of rain, we were advised to sing. For me, however, the upbeat messages in these tunes came across as threats: "I want to be happy/But

I won't be happy/Till I make you happy, too." The sour face with which I greeted these songs of joy never met with any punishment, much to my mother's credit, as I was the baby of the family and therefore afforded the luxury of cynicism. Once out of the house, however, I began my own collection. It was the early seventies when I went away to college, and in those days the antidote to Doris Day was Leonard Cohen. On the cover of my first album is a young girl being burned alive. A dark-eyed beauty, a kind of a Jewish Joan of Arc, is engulfed in Bible-red flames. Chained and manacled, she will never be allowed even a metaphorical escape. Her head tilted upward, she pleads for death, the look on her face not unlike the look on the singer-songwriter's own wife's face, who, it was rumored at the time, committed suicide by crawling into the ground floor of an elevator shaft, lying face up, and waiting for the elevator car to come down and crush her.

You've got it on the wrong speed, numbskull.

I had come to college with my girlhood record player, the kind that folds up like a suitcase so you can take it on slumber parties. It had three settings—33 ⅓ for the parents' records, 45 for my sister's, and 78 for my own yellow Disneys. I gave my roommate Terry Perry a look saying I was no numbskull—in fact I had come to college in a concerted family effort to allay said stigma—but right is right, so I switched the speed up from 45 to 78. She rolled her eyes as far back into her beautiful brainy head as they would go—Terry Perry was a physics major and a violinist for the university orchestra, second chair, a coup for a freshman—got up out of her beanbag chair, came over and turned Leonard down to his correct, if funereal, 33 ⅓ drone, and thus begat the litany of death that was to become my record collection. Marianne Faithfull came with her own razor blade. Patsy Clorox-on-the-rocks Cline, anyone? I acquired all the love minus zero, no limit to my self-loathing Dylania, de-1971-rigueur, *Tapestry*—I was, after all, a girl—and then the classic, the death wish for the lovelorn, that is Joni Mitchell's *Blue*. No self-respecting collection of mortality could be, of course, without the king, the *roi,* Roy Orbison. Not the "Oh, Pretty Woman" Roy but the Roy of *In Dreams,* the record he made after his wife and child burned up in a fire. It is on this album his voice gets that spooky operatic quality, that sublime beatified death rattle. Photographs of him from this point on show the color in his eyes as it drains to pink. Then, one day, behind his thick black signature frames, he simply disappears. She was the only woman he would ever truly love, his real-life mystery girl. Terry Perry called me a romantic dumb-ass and got me Mahler's Third. Talk about a sad sack—Mahler, not Terry. At the time, Terry was working on Mendelssohn's Violin Concerto, and to her Mahler was a lightweight, perfect for a music appreciation beginner like me. Today if you asked me, I would say it is the Mahler that speaks to the tiny green velvet compartment that is my better soul, but at the time it was Mendelssohn. I was eighteen years old. I had neither loved nor lost, but listening to the Mendelssohn, I felt all love, all loss. Grief minus zero, no limit. I would come home from French and plant myself in the hall outside our dormitory door, forgetting the *plus-que-parfait du subjonctif des verbes être et avoir,* while Terry Perry sawed away at the history of grief. Our next-door neighbors growing up had a mango tree in their backyard and were Catholic and therefore weird, so I thought the Billie Holiday song called "Strange Fruit" was a ballad addressed to a mango.

IT'S A LYNCHING, EINSTEIN, Terry Perry informs me. IN THE HISTORY OF SONG, IT MAY VERY WELL BE THE MOST PERFECT GARDENIAED INDICTMENT OF MAN'S INHUMANITY TO MAN.

OH, says I, flipping a page in my *National Geographic,* a subscription to which, along with a Bible, my parents had sent me to college with.

Oh, and my George Jones! How could I forget my beloved George Jones? I moved out of the dorm into an apartment with Eddie Farmer, my first real boyfriend. Eddie was the TA for my philosophy class, Reasoning and Critical Thinking. He already had a master's in linguistics when I met him, but I still had to explain to him that the reason "He Stopped Loving Her Today" was because he was dead.

THEY PUT A WREATH UPON HIS DOOR, ASSHOLE. WHAT DO YOU THINK THAT MEANS, IT'S CHRISTMAS?

Eddie was a generous guy and kind. He had been raised in Tampa by Methodists, so he just smiled and patted the sofa cushion next to him for me to come over and sit down. He had not been raised on Doris Day and therefore had no need for an antidote to happiness. He was raised on Mario Lanza and had always known somehow the world would be a little sad. The day we moved in together, his father sent us a housewarming present of whiskey he had made himself on his own little squat farm in the Florida sticks. It came in a heavy glass bottle the shape of a log cabin. One sip and you were on Mars. I think Eddie was the only boy who ever truly loved me, because whenever he had to go out of town, he would hide from me my George Jones and our little log cabin before leaving.

NO WONDER YOU WANT TO KILL YOURSELF, Lydia said the first time she saw my record collection. LOOK AT ALL THIS DROOPY-DRAWERS MUSIC.

She went out and got me Little Richard's *Greatest Hits,* and that afternoon life began to look up. As it turns out, I have a naturally sunny disposition. I like to watch sports on TV. I like to play cards, canasta mostly, but pinochle sometimes too. I like to talk about my hair and what can be done about it. I have grown extremely fond of this Doris Day.

I have to hand it to my mother. After all these years, I think I'm beginning to understand. There's a lot to be said for pointless optimism.

They met on a railroad track just outside of Kokomo.

There was a yellow school bus full of children stalled on the tracks. He was eighteen and in his father's borrowed Buick. He jumped out of the car. Lydia was in the car behind, our mother at the wheel wondering what in the world, probably one of those teenage pranks, what do they call it? Chinese fire drill? But it was no joke. There was a school bus full of children and the train was coming and the bus was stalled.

He pushed and he pushed and finally, impossibly, he pushed the bus across the tracks. All the children were saved.

People got out of their cars and Mother said who is that? and Lydia said that's Danny Farguson. He's senior class president. He plays the drums.

So well, in fact, did he play the drums, that he won an ROTC scholarship to Ball State University. The scholarship went to whichever student won the Senior Talent Show Contest. Danny got up on stage wearing nothing but black. He had talked the school principal into letting him turn off all the lights at assembly, even though that went against every regulation in the book, young man. He disappeared behind his drums and began to play. You couldn't see anything because the lights were off and Danny was all in black. The only thing you could see were his sticks. He had dipped his drumsticks three times into three different cans of colored neon paint: yellow caution, orange danger, perfect pink. It was 1964 in high school, Indiana.

Wipe out.

That day at the railroad tracks, Danny had not been so busy saving the lives of children that he did not notice a beautiful girl when he saw one. Even though he was a senior and Lydia a sophomore, it didn't matter. They began to meet every Sunday after church, secretly, by the tetherball pole. The tetherball pole was perfect, because, although there were a lot of kids there on Sunday, nobody in Indiana actually plays tetherball, so they had the spot to themselves. Of course, I knew everything. When Lydia's in love, she irons hard. Now she ironed her blouse like crazy. Sometimes, in her hurry to see Danny, she would leave the spray starch out. Leaving the can of spray starch out was the only really bad thing my sister ever did, growing up.

Who left the Faultless out? my mother would say.

Then Danny started calling. When the phone rang, Lydia seemed to know when it was him. She'd call for me to pick it up and then dive into the bathroom to brush her teeth. I stalled Danny as long as it took, noting privately that my sister had gone completely insane. Finally, he came for Sunday dinner, and that was that. They saw each other nonstop that summer; then we got stationed in France. Danny went to Ball State, in Muncie, on his drum scholarship and became a rotzie. Danny and Lydia wrote letters back and forth to each other for two solid years. The first Christmas, he sent Lydia a Bible with her name on it. We all knew then it was the real thing. The Bible had a white leather cover with a pretty gold zipper going all around it, like a girl's diary. Her name was inscribed in gold at the bottom. LYDIA ANN LINDLEY.

In France, Lydia turned sixteen, seventeen, and eighteen. She graduated from high school and was accepted at SMU, where she planned to become a nurse. The minute she got back to the States, she and Danny got engaged, and then, after a year went by, they got married in a tiny Methodist church in Tampa, out by the dog tracks. It has a small steeple that lights up at night. You can see it from the Interstate when you're driving by.

The wedding was fancy. Mother made the bridesmaids' gowns. I got to be one of the bridesmaids, which was exciting, as I was fourteen and had never been on stage before. I helped stain the lace. We filled the washing machine up with hot water and put in a box of teabags, then the lace. I was fearful Dad would see what we were doing and, at the very least, take my Teen Club card away.

We had not gotten the Air Force generic brand, but
Lipton: an entire box, a summer's worth of iced tea,
down the drain. Mother assured me she had squared it
with our father the night before. Still, as soon as the lace
was set, she had me take the evidence—the emptied
Lipton box and the used teabags—out of the house and
down the street to the school dumpster, in case the sight
of such waste reinvigorated his protestations. Then we
did the sugar cubes. Two hundred sugar cubes had to be
decorated, each with a red rose made out of cake icing on
top. My sister had seen it in a magazine. It took two sep-
arate cake bowls; we needed red for the rose and green for
the two dots of green on either side, which my sister
insisted would result in the verisimilitude she was trying
to effect. The sugar cubes were set on the table with a
hundred-cup stainless steel coffee urn Mother got from
the church. Nobody used the sugar cubes, of course. Poor
people know the difference between what is useful, in
life, and what is just for show. I burned quietly, inside,
from the effort spent on something so pointless and
began, for the first time in my life, to align myself with
our penny-pinching father. The rehearsal dinner was held
in the fanciest restaurant in Tampa, the Kapok Tree Inn.
The Kapok Tree Inn was really an inn with a restaurant
attached to it. There was a big kapok tree out front where
you walk in. For two weeks in the spring, when the tree
blooms, the flowers are luminescent, so that the tree looks

as if it's beset with fireflies. In Malaysia, where the kapok grows wild, they use the silky mass of fibers that clothe the seeds of the tree to make stuffing for mattresses, sleeping bags, insulation, and life preservers.

After the wedding, Danny joined the Air Force and at the age of twenty-six became the youngest second lieutenant in the history of the Air Force. He flew C-130s, cargo planes that bring, among other things, refugee children into the states from countries all over the world. When he was on TDY in Taipei, his squadron started an orphanage for the kids who'd been left behind, for one reason or another, by their servicemen dads. Danny got special permission from the base commander, and he and his buddies built it on their off time. Once they got the roof up, the first thing Danny did was put in a stove and a refrigerator and start making Sunday morning pancakes for the kids. One of his buddies was from California and knew how to burnish wood. He made a big sign out of a two-by-four that said DANNY'S INTERNATIONAL HOUSE OF PANCAKES. He nailed the sign above the front door as a joke, but they kept it up. It was a six-month TDY, but the wives were only allowed to come over once. When Lydia got there, the first thing she wanted to do was visit the kids. They had been married for five years. She and Danny spent all day in the orphanage, and by the end of her two-week visit they had decided which two kids they were going to adopt. One was a girl and one was a boy, brother and sister. They would start with these two, then go on to have their own. Danny wanted a football team and Lydia wanted the cheerleaders. When Lydia made the announcement, our father was elated. Before, when Lydia came home for a visit, he would go in her train case and throw away her birth control pills. Lydia would wake up in the morning and have to dig her birth control pills out of the wastepaper basket in the bathroom. It was embarrassing that her father would actually go into her train case. Lydia was so modest. She and Danny had been engaged for a year before she allowed him to take off his shirt in front of her. I remember the day because it was the day I had just learned how to play "Flow Gently, Sweet Afton" on our new Hammond organ that Mom babysat for a thousand hours in order to buy. I bet Danny fifty cents I could play it all the way through without making a mistake, and I played it all the way through without making a mistake, and he gave me fifty cents.

Danny spent six months in Taipei. The night before he was set to come home, he was stabbed forty-seven times and left lying in an alley behind a row of American bars called the Dirty Dozen. He was twenty-seven years old. Lydia was twenty-five. No explanation was ever given. Lydia received three letters from the commander of the Air Force. The first said what an outstanding individual Danny was, and spoke of all the good he had done. The second said they arrested a man. And in the third letter, the commander informed Lydia that the man was a local, meaning a nationalist Chinese, and the Chinese court had given him a sentence of fifteen years. Again, the commander wished to express his deepest sympathy during this time of sadness. After six years, the man was released, whereupon he emigrated to the United States. He now lives in Boston, where he has made something of himself, opening a Chinese restaurant, steps away from the entrance to the quad at a highly rated university. It's an excellent location, and there is a steady clientele. From everything we hear, he is doing pretty well.

✳ ✳ ✳

Part Two: Ancient History

Your chairs. Oh, my.

She's here. In my house. My sister.

They are perfection.

As is she. I take her hat and bag and put them in her room. A hat! In Chicago! Not a rain hat or a snow hat or a protect-yourself-from-the-cold hat. Just a hat. For fun. *Quelle idée!* I come back out to the living room, where she is petting my three kittens. I always forget how beautiful my sister is. In elementary school she was the Gasparilla

Queen, and in high school the Homecoming. Her beauty is a simple fact, like tree trunks. But there is good beautiful and bad beautiful and my sister is good beautiful. I pour champagne into Flintstone jelly glasses and hand her the Wilma. I am completely happy. My sister is here, and because my sister is here I am somehow more me. It's as if all the things *I* think about me get together with all the things *she* thinks about me, and the two of them play well together.

VERY NICE, she says about the champagne.

TOO YEASTY?

MAYBE A TAD.

Delicate palate does not begin to describe what my sister has. Me, I buy Tabasco sauce by the quart, get it home, and pour it into a big Tupperware icewater pitcher. I like it on my morning scrambled, but what I don't like is for Ricky to see my underarm chicken flap, so the pitcher works perfectly, serving both my purposes, allowing for the quantity I like and at the same time ensuring that Ricky never sees those giant shaking hams. Lydia, on the other hand, blindfolded, can pick out a green M&M from every other. I spent my childhood testing her, using the pink belt to our mother's bathrobe for the blindfold. IT's A GREEN, she would say, spitting it out. *It tastes like soap, are you trying to kill me?* Other childhood entertainments included sitting in the backyard looking for four-leaf clovers (Lydia always found one), teaching the cat to wink (Lydia performed this miracle), touching tongues (don't ask), and playing Don't Smile. To this day, Lydia can look at me at a funeral and say "Don't smile" and I will throw my head back and laugh like an ugly blonde hyena.

I watch my sister take a seat in the Abortion Chair.

Instead of a couch, I have three big chairs. There is the Abortion Chair, the Florida Grandma Chair, and My Funny Valentimes Chair. (Ricky can't say *valentine*.) The Abortion Chair is, actually, the most comfortable of the three. My student Shine made it out of coat hangers.

A LITTLE DECONSTRUCTION GOES A LONG WAY, I said, AT ART SCHOOL.

HIPPIE PARENTS? asks Lydia.

CONNECTICUT HIPPIE.

The seat is way high up, so Lydia has to give a little hop to get on it, and a pretty little hop it is. Her feet just barely graze the floor. The chair, according to Shine, is based on an ancient Egyptian birthing chair, a design she found in a picture book on midwifery. Sitting straight up is thought to be one of the more comfortable positions to give birth in. She got the coat hangers from a neighborhood dry cleaner, a thousand for a buck. She put them out on her back stoop all winter long, till they rusted red. In the spring, she dipped them in a solvent that melded the rust to the metal and then put them on wax paper to dry. It took two more weeks for that to happen. Then came the hard part, coaxing each hardened hanger, without losing the beautiful red rusted bits, into this, a mesh of metastasized metal. The chair goes all the way up to the ceiling. It looks like a chair Modigliani might have made, were he having a really bad day. Say he was feeling particularly lonely that day, this is the chair he would have come up with. It's a red throne for a blue queen.

It's got gravity going for it, says Lydia. I like it.

I take a seat in my gooseneck rocker, my Florida Grandma, a happy tapestry of teacup hibiscus and flamingo-pink magnolias.

Do you want a shower or anything? There's plenty of time—our reservation's not till eight; how Paris is that?

That is so very Paris. I don't know. Bored with me, already? How about we just sit?

I point to My Funny Valentimes chair. That one's my favorite.

It is an aluminum lawn chair, the fold-out kind, a full-length recliner. It's buried in hundreds of tiny heart-shaped beanbags: pillowed conversation hearts, lentils in velvet, each carrying its own red-stitched message: kiss me. i like you. be mine.

Ricky sounds like a nice guy, says Lydia.

I give it a year, I say, pouring myself more champagne. We laugh, both knowing how bad I am at love.

He can't say your name.

He can't say Lydia?

This morning he was all "Libya is coming! Libya is coming!" I told him if Libya is coming, we better get more chairs.

Well, I don't care. I like him. I believe I would enjoy being an African nation.

Meanwhile, my three kittens, who have made a white nest in Lydia's lap, give me looks of reproach. Why didn't you tell us she was this nice, Mommy? We would have cleaned the house all by ourselves.

To the squirrel, I say, raising my glass. Now how did I wind up with the Barney? I hate the Barney.

Lydia raises her glass to mine and we clink. She knows I'm dying to tell my squirrel story. She can tell it is a story full of entanglement, complication, denouement— maybe two. There will be explication, historical and emotional, and backups. I am certain to forget to tell the most important thing first, one of my less pleasing qualities. But Lydia thinks it is a story best kept for the restaurant and I do not disagree. It is a story for after: after all the decisions have been made—what wine, which entrées, how many appetizers. I look at her. My sister would just like to sit for a while, if she may. She is not interested right now in a story about a squirrel.

You still get these old things? she asks, smiling, as she sets Wilma down on the coffee table and picks up the *National Geographic* on top.

Thank God I remembered.

The last thing I did before going to bed last night was to put the top *Geographic* on the bottom. Hsing-Hsing died last month, the National Zoo's last remaining giant panda. They put him on the cover.

The article, inside, recounts his life. Hsing-Hsing and his mate, Ling-Ling, arrived at the National Zoo in green lacquered crates on April 16, 1972, accompanied by armed guards. The gift was a happy by-product of Nixon's historic visit to China, and the animals were an immediate hit with the public. Attention turned quickly to the possibility of a baby panda, but it was not to be. Hsing-Hsing lived to be twenty-seven, an advanced age, they say, for a panda.

It was on the way to see Hsing-Hsing that I discovered my sister's eyes turned blue.

Lydia moved to Hawai'i after Danny died. The Air Force had given her a lump sum, because when you die in the service you get a lump sum. She bought a little yellow sports car and a Boston Whaler and drove across country from Tallahassee to Los Angeles to the Rose Bowl, to see USC beat the pants off Michigan. At the entrance to the Rose Bowl she bought a tin medal pin that said MUCK FICHIGAN, which shocked even her. She had never said a bad word in her life, not even *barf*. But she was beginning to change. After the game, she drove to Long Beach, where she loaded the car and the boat and herself on a transport ship. A guy offered to paint the gas cap on her car for free and Lydia said Why not? He painted a picture of a blue sea and a blue sky. There were seagulls in it. At the bottom of the picture, he painted her name in tiny blue letters: LYDIA ANN.

When she got to Hawai'i, she found a place to live and began looking for something to do. She got a job in the children's section of the public library in Honolulu, where she built a saltwater aquarium. She took scuba lessons and began a collection. Each day, she added to the tank. Ask my sister anything about life in saltwater, because she can tell you. She has become an expert on shells.

Six months went by and Lydia called, wondering if I would go with her to Arlington. She wanted to go see the headstone, which had not been ready on the day of the funeral. I said Sure, and why don't we see a little of the DC area while we're at it? I had an ex-boyfriend in the symphony who could get us tickets, and another who worked at the Folger who could get us a discount in the museum shop. I think Ray is still at the Library of Congress. We can get a behind-the-scenes tour.

PLUS, I said, I'D LOVE TO SEE THOSE PANDAS AT THE NATIONAL ZOO.

HAVE AN EX-BOYFRIEND THERE, TOO? asked Lydia.

HOW MANY TIMES DO I HAVE TO TELL YOU? IT WAS THE SEVENTIES.

Ray's office was a tiny cell. He had just given us a swell tour of the library-behind-the-library. It was like the catacombs, one topic per cell. Ray's topic was gospel. He was in charge of knowing everything that could be known about gospel music in America. He had sheet music stacked to the ceiling like notational stalagmites. His specialty, sacred steel, was a category of music I had never heard of, but Lydia had. Poor churches in small Florida towns that didn't have enough for an organ used, as their orchestral accompaniment on Sundays, whoever was walking through that part of the world that day who could play steel guitar. Patrons of these churches, instead of asking what the sermon would be about this week, asked the preacher, Who's on steel? People walked miles just to hear their favorite player, like—

SONNY TREADWAY? said Lydia.

YOU KNOW SONNY TREADWAY? Ray looked at my sister, a little more admiringly than I would have liked.

Lydia and Ray got to talking Sonny Treadway and suddenly they're the old pals of yore and I'm the sad sister who just lost the only man she would ever in this world love. It took me awhile to convince Ray that he had a lot of work to do, and besides, Lydia and I had a date with a couple of pandas. But we missed Hsing-Hsing and Ling-Ling. We made it to the National Zoo, but the giant pandas were nowhere in sight. We hung around, until, finally, someone went to ask. We were told they were depressed.

That seemed weird to me. Pandas don't get depressed; they're cute. They are funny and whimsical and happy and cute, and Hsing-Hsing and Ling-Ling are the two most beloved pandas on earth! What do they have to be depressed about?

We took the bus back to the hotel, and that's when I noticed.

Lydia ann Lindley! You big cheater, you!

Lydia, her whole life, has told me she wished her eyes were blue like mine. Her eyes are green. I liked knowing there was something I had that she wanted. But she must have gotten colored contacts to make her eyes look blue. She'd done it the phony way.

Watch what you wish for, sweet pea, she said. You know that old saying?

I didn't believe her. I scooted over in my seat and looked straight in, searching for the telltale rounds of the contacts. But no luck. Maybe it was living in Hawaii—all that clean air and blue water. She spent all day long, after all, in the deep blue sea. Maybe eyes turn blue when they are finally clean. Or after they have been immersed in blue water for a very long period of time. But, Lydia told me no. She said she just cried till they turned blue.

* * *

Part Three: The Perfect Restaurant

I KNEW YOU'D FIND THE PERFECT RESTAURANT.

Nothing could be more gratifying to my ears than these sweet words of acknowledgment from my big sister. We had arrived half an hour early, which was fine by me. I've been known to go to the airport the night before a flight out. But finding my sister the perfect restaurant had not been easy. Problem number one, Lydia is a gourmet. I used to tell people my sister had penultimate taste before one of my students corrected me. I thought penultimate meant the ultimate of ultimate. But like Ricky says, live and learn!

Lord knows where she got it from. We were raised on hamburger steak with Worcestershire sauce for gravy, and the only dessert we had ever known was mayonnaise cake. Eggs and oil were expensive in World War II, so our Grandma Ada got the idea to use mayonnaise, because mayonnaise was cheap. It is a heavy chocolate cake and, actually, delicious. Just don't say what it is you're making if they're not in the family. Our family has made mayonnaise cake the same way since day one, until Lydia. Lydia discovered an extract of lemon in Miracle Whip that gave it a quality she found delightful, so she began making it with Miracle Whip. Thank goodness, Grandma Ada never found out. She died a peaceful death in her pretty bed in Tampa.

The only other delicacy our family could lay claim to was a tiny glass of corned beef in water our father kept in the refrigerator behind the little hinged door where the butter is supposed to go. This was his personal treat and it remained guarded behind the butter door, like a thing in a museum. My sister and I used to scare ourselves silly by saying out loud all the things our dad would do to us if we so much as touched that little corned beef in a glass.

Still, somehow Lydia grew up to have a very delicate palate. She has been everywhere, with everyone, in the finest of all places, so when she first called to say she was coming to Chicago, I put Charlie Trotter's at the top of the list. I had to cross it off almost immediately, though. I don't mind spending the rent on a nice meal, but this was to be her treat. Besides, I heard he's moving to Spain, a place with colors in it. All these years I have thought Chicago was to blame for why Lydia never came to visit. I can understand how it is not the first place one thinks of when one thinks vacation. When Lydia goes on vacation, she goes to Hawaii, another place with colors in it.

Problem number two is the fact that Lydia cannot abide anything the least bit spicy. She refuses all Thai, Chinese, and Indian food, which of course are my three favorites and why I have conveniently forgotten to tell her the chef at the restaurant we are at tonight was trained in Hong Kong.

Then there's the other problem.

PLEASE, DON'T SAY IT OUT LOUD, LYDIE. IT'S SO EMBARRASSING.

BUT I AM A VEGETARIAN.

Lydia grew up when meat meant red meat, and because she does not eat red meat she thinks she's a vegetarian. She eats pork, chicken, fish, duck and lamb. Veal. Liverwurst, if you put it on a cracker with mayonnaise. Rabbit, that time in Paris. I've seen her eat a snake—well, she took a bite. Aunt Lois made appetizers once out of a fried snake her cave son Weldon had caught. She put toothpicks in and set them on the table and they were gone in an instant though everybody said later they thought it was Vienna sausages. Our family was relieved when they caught the Unabomber, as we had always assumed it was our cave cousin Weldon.

WELL, she conceded, I AM AND I AMN'T.

The restaurant doesn't even have a name, how cool is that? It isn't even a restaurant, it's the dining part of an inn. You have to call the inn part to make a reservation. The chef comes to your table and talks to you and asks you about things you like, and then he goes and fixes you something he thinks you'll enjoy. No waiters! Just a man and his pan. On the cab ride over, my sister and I rehearsed what we would say. You just make whatever you feel like making, and I will love it, is what I was going to say. The hotter the better!

THE OPPOSITE OF THAT is what my sister will say.

We are opposites, my sister and I. I have clothes; Lydia has outfits. Lydia cleans soft and I clean hard. When I'm done cleaning, the house looks defeated, but when Lydia cleans, it's fucking Beauty and the Beast in there, the teacups dancing. Let us help! they cry. We promise never to get dirty again! When it comes to money, my sister is the ant and I'm the grasshopper. When retirement day comes around, she will have a choice: Italy or Hawaii? I, too, will have a choice: Write a bad check at the Piggly-Wiggly or at Albertson's for the catfood that is beginning to taste not bad over a baked potato? And when the end of the world does finally come, when we are holed up in that final underground bunker, a place I imagine to be like the cellar in *The Wizard of Oz* where Dorothy and her family huddle while the tornado passes overhead, Lydia, the cellar's elected queen, will quietly scold me, the sorrowful sad sack who predicted the whole thing, who told you so, who told you once and told you twice if you voted for the Shrub this would one day happen. Lydia will put her hand on my shoulder, hunched over in the corner, turning the pages of my Leonard Cohen novel, turn to the others, and say, You know what would taste really, really good right now? A nice tall glass of apricot nectar. A blue crystal glass, with lots and lots of shaved ice. Then, while people begin to fight over who will have the privilege of going out into the post-nuclear air, I will be still. I'll say, You know, I'm not sure that's such a good idea. They say the air is supposed to be kind of bad for you. Everybody stops fighting. They shut up and turn around and look at me. What a little warner! You know, it wouldn't hurt if you could be a little more positive, like your sister. And the truth is, what will happen is, somebody will go out and will, in fact, find the last tiny can of apricot nectar on earth and a blue crystal glass to put it in and lots and lots of shaved ice. They will return unharmed, healthier even than when they left, and there'll be a party, and everyone will be laughing and saying what a good idea this was, and they'll look at me, the party pooper, and shake their heads. Poor thing. Poor little droopy-drawer thing.

To MY SISTER, says Lydia.

To MY SISTER, says I.

We had polished off the wine and had to clink our water

glasses. Dessert was on its way. It had been a fabulous wine, one of those revelatory wines that changes your mind about wine, making you understand for the first time in your life why people say wine is food. Lydia had chosen it, knowing as she did my propensity for reading a wine list in the Hebraic manner. It was a merlot, which shocked me. I had always understood merlot to be a mutt wine, a give-up wine, a combination of grapes with the misfortune of having had to grow up on the wrong side of the family orchard. But Lydia said merlots can be lovely. Just make sure it's at least three years old and then have at it. I look at her now. I am completely relaxed. Ricky was right. What was all the fuss about? Why had I been so anxious about this visit? Why was I so sure nothing would go right? That nothing would be ready in time—me, the house, the linens, the bathroom tile? Why did I worry so about what restaurant to take her to? Why did I always behave as though the next thing, whatever that thing was, would be a disaster?

IT'S NICE TO SEE YOU, said Lydia, so—

BRIGHT AND SHINY? I KNOW.

IT'S FUNNY. YOU WERE SUCH A NEGATIVE LITTLE KID.

I WANTED PEOPLE TO THINK I WAS AN INTELLECTUAL, I GUESS.

THAT WASN'T TOO HARD IN OUR FAMILY. AS I RECALL, YOU GOT A LOT OF CREDIT FOR BEING THE FIRST TO FIGURE OUT WHAT IT WAS BILLY JOE MCALLISTER THREW OFF THE TALLAHATCHEE BRIDGE.

This was true. It was a baby, right?

I HAD TO BE THE SMART ONE. YOU WERE THE BEAUTY.

I HATE WHEN YOU SAY THINGS LIKE THAT. YOU *ARE*—

OH, SAVE IT. I'M OLD. WHERE'S MY GINGER PUDDING?

IT'S NOT PUDDING.

I HATE SAYING FLAN. IT'S SO FINAL. IT'S SO FLANNEL. FLAN. IT SOUNDS LIKE THE NAME OF THE NEIGHBOR LADY WHO TAKES CARE OF YOUR CATS. YOU KNOW, FLAN. THE ONE DOWN THE ROAD WITH THE DRINKING PROBLEM?

SWEET PEA. IT MUST BE SO HARD BEING YOU. HOW DOES RICKY MANAGE?

HE LOVES IT. THEY USUALLY DO THE FIRST YEAR.

Lydia's right. I was a serious kid, so serious it must've been funny. I looked around the family supper table one night, and there they all were. Angry at the head of the table, eating his beloved creamed corn straight out of the can. Exhaustion, the tiny blonde thing, sat at the other end, trying her best to make the mashed potatoes go farther than they could ever possibly go in the world. And there was Beauty, sitting right across from me, and even though I was ten years old I knew I would never be beautiful like my sister, so, I decided to be Deep. Deep and sad, sad and deep. I was the saddest, deepest, most miserable monkey I could possibly be. Look, my mother said, the Eiffel Tower! How deep, I thought, how sad. Over there, she said, the Colosseum! It was a perfect Easter day. Very sad, I thought, so deep. In college, it was even easier to be deep and sad. I dated musicians, I drank anything yellow, I majored in literature. I walked all over campus with *Being and Nothingness* under my arm as proof of just how deep and sad I was. I read Kierkegaard with no understanding, Wittgenstein. I signed up for the philosophy of everything. I stood in line for every film about nothingness a university film center could offer. The more nothing, the better. There was one Warhol film about a crane on top of a building. Forty-four minutes. You watch the basket of the crane on the building go up. Then down. Up, down. Up, down. This was deep. This was sad.

Finally, the real thing. The cino-death-trip dream come true. Fritz Lang, the Retrospective. Monday night, *Die Nibelungen,* Part One: the death of Siegfried. The hero bathes in the blood of a dragon he has just slain. He marries a princess, but wicked Queen Brünnhilde has him killed. Message? Death is inevitable. Tuesday night, Part Two: Siegfried's widow marries Attila the Hun. Message? Death is inevitable.

DO YOU REMEMBER MY BOYFRIEND RONNY?

THEY HAD NAMES?

OH THAT'S SO FUNNY, I FORGOT TO LAUGH. PIANO RONNY. YOU REMEMBER RONNY. MR. SAY-NOTHING?

ELECTRIC OR ACOUSTIC?

AT LEAST TRY. ELECTRIC PIANO IS SO EIGHTIES.

HE THE ONE WITH THE OXYGEN TANKS?

Ronny, the boyfriend du jour, was my one musician

with a job. He made fifty dollars whenever the university film center showed a silent film and needed the organ or piano played. I was his page turner. I didn't read music, so he tied a string around my right thigh and his left thigh, and when it was time for a page to be turned, he gave a little tug. After each movie, we went to the Mecca, the college coffeehouse, where we would order something to drink and sit there and not drink it. We would sit, stir, and stare. Ronny was usually the first to stir. He would stir, put his spoon down, and stare. Now it was my turn. I tried to be philosophical about it, as philosophical as any nineteen-year-old girl with nothing on her mind could be. I stirred, stared, and stirred again. When I stared up, Ronny stared down. When Ronny stared up, it was my turn to stare down. Sometimes, we would stare together in the same direction. I felt close to him then. It was the kind of deep and sad I was always looking for, in a film or a boy. Eventually, one of us would have to say something, usually Ronny. He would tilt his head and chair back, open his mouth, and let the air out, as if he were a tortured flat tire.

DEATH, BABE. IT'S JUST SO FUCKING INEVITABLE.

Finally. We could go back to his place and have sex. Tomorrow, we would live to be sad and deep again.

RICKY CAN'T EVEN SAY THE WORD *INEVITABLE*. I THINK THAT'S ONE REASON I LIKE HIM SO MUCH.

WHAT DOES HE SAY?

HE SAYS *IN-EVI-VABLE*. THEN HE KIND OF GIGGLES.

THAT RICKY IS ADORABLE. WHY DID HE HAVE TO GO TO SEATTLE AGAIN?

I tell her why again, and she says what a shame, and that the next time she comes she would really like to meet him. She seems to really mean it. That she would come a next time.

We exchange our minor-league success stories. Her pre-school was voted one of the top ten preschools in Hollywood. I got a faculty grant from school to translate *Peau d'Ane,* a French fairy tale about incest. In rhymed verse.

TRY FINDING A WORD IN ENGLISH THAT RHYMES WITH "DONKEY SKIN," I say. FOR STARTERS.

She tells me about one of her kids, Angela, who wrote a poem about a spider who was a good spider and saved a boy from drowning in a big blue swimming pool. I tell her Shine had her first CD come out. It is on the Shit Fuck & Die label, a local label but a good one. Her band is called The New Christy Menstruals.

A strand of hair has fallen down the side of Lydia's face. It was not something she'd meant to happen. She had her hair up in a pretty pony knot at the top of her head and she meant for it all to be up there. She starts in on her next story, this one about Nicholas, her favorite student— it's a kite story. I reach over and take the strand of hair and push it back up into her pony knot where it belongs and then it comes to me. Lil Dagover. That was the name of the actress I was trying to drum up but couldn't when I was telling my Ronny story.

Dagover was Fritz Lang's favorite actress, I guess. If I'm not mistaken, she was in every one of his films, my favorite being *Destiny,* the scene at the beginning, anyway. *Destiny* was Lang's first international hit. The German, *Der Müde Tod,* "Weary Death," was a bit much for 1920s America, so they cheered it up a bit, preferring to translate it as *Destiny.* Death does not seem so inevitable if one has destiny. The French, those wise apples, got four more people to the theater by calling it *The Three Candles,* possibly one of the more heinous cases of false advertising in the history of film titles. The film is a dark little movie. Death is weary. After all, it is post–World War I and, in Germany, Lil and Fritz are practically the only two people left standing. In a fairy tale atmosphere, Death comes dressed in a cape to claim a young bridegroom, recently married, but because he, Death, is so worn out with all the dying, he makes a bargain with the bride, Dagover. If she can find a single someone in the history of the world who can escape him, Death, her husband may live. You get the feeling even Death needs a breather, at this point in time. He is sick of himself, his job, and the kind of life he is leading, so he takes his cape off, sits down, and watches.

Lil makes three tries, choosing present-day Baghdad, renaissance Venice, and ancient China. There are three different young men in three different life-threatening circumstances. In one scene in the China adventure, a girl and her magician father open a tiny little case and real horses jump out.

But the scene I'm thinking of is the scene at the beginning. Lil and her new husband stop for lunch at a country inn. There is a big beautiful tree outside. They go in and are seated, and the manager of the inn, upon hearing they are newlyweds, comes over to serve them wine out of the special newlywed cup. It's a cool cup, an ingenious two-headed gadget that allows both man and wife to drink out of the same vessel at the same time. The girl gets the smaller portion, but what the hey— what do you want?—this is 1921. Then it happens. The girl excuses herself from the table and goes to find the ladies' room. She passes through the lobby, where someone has left a basket of kittens. She goes over to pet the kittens, and while she's literally pussyfooting around, Death strolls in behind her back and takes her honey away.

So. Let's have it.

Have what.

Your squirrel story.

Lydia was having a nice time, I could tell. She seemed funny when we first got to the restaurant, but after a little wine and six happy courses of beautiful food she kept remarking on, I think she was finally relaxed and comfortable being in a strange town with her little sister.

Go.

I had despaired of ever coming up with the perfect restaurant for Lydia, when voilà! the squirrel literally fell out of the clear blue sky and landed in front of the guy's car. Ricky was working at the Clark Street Animal Hospital and was in the office when the guy ran in with the bleeding squirrel, his little daughter in tow. The guy looked to be a weekend dad or a stepdad. Either way, it seemed extremely important to him to look good in front of this little girl. Ricky told me the father hadn't killed the squirrel, but that the squirrel had probably fallen off a telephone wire. It had been dead for a while. The father brought the squirrel in for a resurrection, or at least a show. Ricky understood this immediately. He can put on a show as good as anybody, when it comes to helping somebody out, and the two men did just that. They attempted a resurrection. Ricky bent over the squirrel and performed "an emergency appendichotomy." After enough time had passed, and when the little girl's interest began to wane, Ricky said they'd have to operate and could the father assist.

He and the father took the squirrel tenderly behind closed doors.

The father was so grateful. He handed Ricky a slip of paper, saying, THIS IS THE BEST-KEPT SECRET IN

CHICAGO. JUST CALL AHEAD AND LET THEM KNOW YOU'RE
COMING. I PROMISE YOU, IT'S THE SINGLE BEST DINING
EXPERIENCE YOU WILL EVER HAVE.

After enough time went by, Ricky and the father came
out. Ricky was in his white lab coat, which lent his lie
authenticity. He told the little girl that despite all her
dad's valiant efforts, after everything that could be done
had been done, the squirrel was in heaven.

Ricky and I never got to go to the restaurant because the
guy didn't say meal, he said experience. Experiences are
expensive. I remain hopeful we will go one day. I try to stay
positive. Did you know that in the eighteenth century the
opposite of positive was not negative but natural? Natural.
What does that mean? I have no idea, I just know it.

Nothing I know does me any good.

Now, everybody I talk to says yes, they've heard of the
place. One of their friends had a friend who went there
but they themselves have never been.

SO YOU THINK MAYBE RICKY'S THE ONE? asked Lydia.

HE'S OKAY.

YOU KNOW, HONEY. YOU'RE ALLOWED.

I KNOW.

YOU DON'T HAVE TO ALWAYS LOSE ON PURPOSE JUST
BECAUSE.

QUIT BEING SO PSYCHOLOGICAL. YOU'RE SO PSYCHO-
LOGICAL THESE DAYS. AND JUST AS OUR PUDDING IS
COMING.

I look up and see the chef approach with our dessert. The entire restaurant is cleared out. We have been here for hours and never even noticed. The dishwasher probably has a date, not to mention the chef. He must be exhausted. Still, he has all evening long been very nice to us. There hasn't been the endless, Will there be anything elses? Not one.

For the lady? He presents my sister with a lovely blue dish of ginger flan. There is a crystallized violet on top. Nice.

Has everything been to your satisfaction? he asks. He is a pleasant fellow, this chef. He has short, intelligent, sticky black hair.

It was a perfect meal, my sister says. May I shake your hand?

The fellow is happy to shake the hand of such a beautiful lady. He smiles big, accepts my sister's hand, and they shake. I have to say I'm beginning to feel a little left out. Shouldn't I be getting at least some of the credit for all this—the beautiful food, the marvelous dessert, the terrific time we are having?

The man returns to the kitchen and my sister picks up her dessert spoon.

Applying for a job? I say.

My sister takes a long, slow, deliberate taste of her pudding, and looks at me.

Sweet pea?

WHAT? I KNOW. I'M SORRY. I'M NOT REALLY—

DEAR HEART. CAN YOU HEAR ME WHEN I SAY TO YOU, YOU HAVE ABSOLUTELY NOTHING—

I KNOW.

I MEAN NOTHING.

And I don't. I know I don't. There is nothing I have to be jealous of.

It's just, I hate people. I especially hate people I do not know. I hate them before they get the first word out. It takes me years to like somebody and even then, once I learn to like them, I still hate them.

It just always amazes me how easy my sister is with people, how loving. How can she be like that?

YOU HAVE NO IDEA WHAT YOU'RE MISSING, she says, tapping her spoon against the pretty blue bowl.

She is right as rain, as usual. The pudding? Powerful. I dig in. It is as if I have never had pudding before. In record time, my bowl is as if new, fresh-from-the-dishwasher clean. I make a mental note to pack a tiny rubber spatula in my purse when Ricky and I come here. If.

I look up. My sister is finished with her dessert. She dabs at each side of her mouth with her dinner napkin, like a kitty cat. I smile, but she doesn't see me. She is not looking up, she is looking down, into her empty dessert bowl. Did the violet fall down into it? No, her dessert bowl really is empty. She's just looking into an empty bowl. I catch her eye. She tries to blink me away,

once, then twice, but I am her sister and therefore I see.
I see the shiver in her eye. It is a look I have seen only
once before.

Robert Daniel Farguson was buried at Arlington Cemetery. The funeral was complete with riderless horse and a
21-gun salute. Lydia wore a pillbox hat with a dotted
Swiss veil that came halfway down her face. She looked
like Jackie Kennedy that day, the hat, the veil, that look
on her face that said *Just keep going.*

But the real funeral, the funeral for Danny Farguson,
was the Indiana funeral in Kokomo. There weren't enough
seats for all the people who came. The organ played while
everyone finally did find a seat, and then the preacher got
up to speak. After some minutes, it became clear he was
the only person in the room who did not know Danny. I
was sitting next to Lydia. I could feel her next to me. She
had twisted her ankle that morning and I looked down
and saw the swelling. Her ankle was purpling and getting
larger and larger with every sentence the preacher deliv-
ered. Nobody believes me when I tell them Lydia used to
be shy as toast, painfully, clinically shy. But as the
preacher continued to talk about this sad tragic end for a
boy so beloved, Lydia began to sit up straighter and
straighter and finally she sat up so straight that she was
standing. The preacher stopped. Then the organist.
Everybody was looking at Lydia. She turned and said,

This is not right. She said, *This is all wrong. Please,* she said. *Everybody. Please go.*

No one moved. And then, one by one, everybody did go. They went kindly. They did what they were asked. It took a while. The preacher came over to Lydia, but she put her arm out so he couldn't get near her. It was the only unkind thing I have ever seen my sister do. I was the last in line to leave the room. Once we were all out, I closed the door behind me to give Lydia her privacy. One last goodbye.

Only I didn't close the door behind me. I started, but as I began to pull the door to I heard a noise. So I stepped back in the room.

Lydia was nowhere to be seen.

Slowly, I walked forward, up to the platform, where the open coffin stood, as if in a dream in which you are made to advance against your will. I reached the stage where the coffin stood and looked down.

Lydie?

She was there, lying beside him. She was twenty-five years old in Kokomo, Indiana.

I can't spit.

She had out her Homecoming handkerchief, baby blue, with a white tiara our mother had stitched into the corner.

I took the handkerchief from her, did my duty, and handed it back. She wiped the side of his cheek, his chin, and then began to work on his hand. They put makeup on him, all the way down, even to his hands.

We worked together, back and forth, for many minutes. We worked well together. We always had. She wiped for a while, then handed me back the handkerchief. I spit, then handed it back to her. We continued in this way until at last the job was done.

Lydie?

I know.

People.

I know.

Ready, now. Take my arm. All set?

She said yes, but I could see the sound in my sister's heart. It was the sound of a metal hook, clanging, faultless, against a tetherball pole.

A Compendium of Skirts

D id *too*," insisted Corrine, twenty-nine and holding, old enough to know better.

"Did too what?" Her husband Michael put his arms around her. His syllables, like his facial features, were not so much even as they were equidistant.

"See Gene Kelly at the Vatican Exhibit today." Corrine stuffed her hands into her skirt pockets and pretended to pout.

They had been walking south, down that part of Michigan Avenue where Chicago suddenly starts trying to act like New York City. They'd just seen *The Thin Man* for the forty millionth time and were now part of the chattering aimless crowd spilling out of the theater, like well-heeled pairs out of a cinematic ark, two by two. Corrine cataloged what she saw. She prided herself on being able to spot first dates; they had that frightened

movie's-over-now-what? look. There were the very well
informed, desperate to discuss their own brand of
psycho-biologies, followed by the overly marrieds with
bad shoes and nothing left to say. Office dates fingered
their ticket stubs deep down in their pockets, embarrassed at having so much free time on their hands, dis-
turbed to have been caught laughing in a public place.
There were city dates, acting as if they had someplace to
go, and out-of-towners clinging to each other instinc-
tively, humbled by the imperturbability of so many
buildings. Here and there were the smiling speechless—
and Corrine counted herself in this category—who, if
only for the nonce, felt a sudden infusion: glad, if only
for the moment, to be a member of this species; grateful,
at any rate, for the sheer human noise.

"Course you did." Michael pointed to a neon café.
"Just like you saw Beckett at the World's Fair. Tea?"

It would be a fair fight.

They crossed Michigan Avenue. She looked at him
from the side while he led the way, skirting possible disaster at every turn—buses, beggars, and money men—
the general rudesby population, heir to a city like this.
His hair was trim, his jacket a perfect fit. The muted gray
tweed of his pants stopped just in time for a couple of
unscuffed Florsheims. Corrine looked down. Her own
limp blonde hair, nowhere near what her mother might
call "fixed," fell haphazardly down, not unlike a blanket

tossed over a floor lamp. It was a cultivated carelessness, she knew. There had been, it occurred to her, a certain concession in his challenge. She needed time to perfect her argument, teaspoon time, and he understood this. And it occurred to her that at this very moment and forever, in kitchens and cafés all over the planet, this argument would continue, back and forth and around and again, conspiratorially or unwittingly, like a sugar bowl passed among guests.

"Men are shits," Jill announced.

"It's not really their fault," put in Annie quickly. "It's just they were raised that way."

"The only way to command the respect of a male of this species is to speak distinctly and in complete sentences," pronounced Elena.

The girls were over. Corrine scrambled eggs while Jill, Annie, and Elena held forth at the kitchen table. Outside, the first snow.

"I *mean*. If the stick brain won't believe you, show him the door. Life's too short." There was an authority in Jill's voice that came from working three jobs. She got up, went over to the sink, and ran hot tap water into her mug. "You got any Lipton? I mean. I'm telling Sam yesterday—no, day before yesterday, Thursday—I'm telling Sam, Sam—"

"That's not what Corrine's talking about, Jill. She

didn't say Michael doesn't *believe* her. It's just he's got this thing where he's got to be *convinced*. Isn't that it, Corrine? That it's, like, symbolic? Symbolic of something bigger?"

"Sort of." Corrine turned the gas down on the eggs. Annie's repertoire worked its way neatly into three categories. There was the Everything Means Something Else conversation, the You've Gotta Do What's Right for You conversation, and the Man Has Not Progressed an Inch Since Lascaux conversation. "Breakfast's ready. Elena, how's your tea? Strong enough?"

"It is." The somber Slavic tone always made Elena sound as if she'd been drugged. Peaches in heavy syrup. She learned English listening to soap operas that blared theatrically through her high ceilings to wherever she happened to be coloring her canvases. That and the Thomas Mann translations she read aloud at night. She didn't talk, she spoke: in sonata form, complete with overture, andante, theme, recapitulation, and coda. If one called her to ask her to a movie, up to forty minutes had to be allotted for her roomy, painstaking reply. She was not windy, just thorough.

"Pass the sugar," Jill said.

Elena passed her the honey. Annie quickly passed her the sugar, not liking an argument.

"Sugar or honey," began Elena, "it comes to much the same thing—a certain adultery. Both spoil, both integrate something of lesser value into what had been. You usurp the purity this way, spoil the original God-smell. In a mere thirty years—"

"I read *Newsweek* too, Elena. Everything's terrible. Fluorescent lights'll make my children short. Your coffee's pure, all right. It's so pure we have to have breakfast at Corrine's 'cause you never Comet out your pot—"

"All right, you two," interrupted Annie. "Corrine honey, you just go on with your story. Jill here was behind—"

"—the barn when God passed out the brains," Jill finished. "Okay, so I don't get it. What's the big deal if Gene Kelly was or wasn't at the thing the other day?"

"Because. I know I exaggerate—okay, lie—but only to . . . okay. I just get tired of having to document everything I say. So when we went to the Vatican Exhibit yesterday—"

"You and Michael."

"Me and Michael."

"By the way, where is Michael?" asked Jill, struck by her powers of observation.

Corrine did not want to tell the girls he was at his mother's helping with the punch. "He's playing football with the office."

"Let Corrine finish," scolded Annie.

"So I'm at this tapestry, you know the one with Jesus in a boat—"

"*The Miraculous Draught of the Fishes,* conceived from

a sketch by Raphael." Elena poured her tea back into the teapot to let it steep longer.

"Right. Right next to the Apollo Belvedere—"

"That's the one with the one arm?"

"Yes. So I'm—"

"How come it's broken—? I mean, if it's damaged—"

"Will you *please?*" Annie sneaked two teaspoons of the white death into her cup.

"So I turn around and there, for the love of the little baby Jesus, is Gene honest-to-God Kelly."

"Gene Kelly, Gene Kelly?"

"I am telling you."

"Pretty wild. Gene Kelly standing there in all that broken art," put in Jill, pleased with her contribution.

"Only I couldn't find Michael. I finally did, three rooms back—he's so pokey when it comes to art—and he's reading this big wall of information about the Egyptians, but by the time we get back to the tapestry room—"

"Gene Kelly is gone."

"And Michael thinks you made it up."

"Well, not exactly. He just wouldn't acknowledge the wonderfulness of it the minute I told him. Later. Later, he finds out there's a Gene Kelly film festival going on, so suddenly there's a reason why Gene Kelly might be in town, and so maybe what I said I saw, I saw. He doesn't believe I saw Beckett at the World's Fair either."

"I didn't know you were in Knoxville," said Annie,

hurt. Her mother still lives in Knoxville and would have been delighted to put Corrine up.

"No, the one in New York."

"How on earth did you know who Samuel Beckett was in 1964?"

"Yeah, you'd only be, maybe—"

"I was ten. My mom, my sister, and my Aunt Margie, we'd all just come out of the Ford Pavilion, and my sister, my sister had this thing for Michelangelo; she'd heard of him, at least, and she's acting wise in front of my aunt— Aunt Margie was sort of the family intellectual, her family had encyclopedias—and besides, I didn't want to see it."

"See what?"

"The Pietà."

"They dragged the Pietà all the—"

"My mom said I didn't have to, I could wait out front on this bench. So that's what I did, and there was a man. His face was like a hawk, only handsome. I fantasized he was there to ask me to marry him—very tragic, as I'd of course have to refuse him, due to 'Father's temperament' and so on. But he just asked me what my name was. I said Esmeralda and I couldn't stay long, because I was 'expected.' He said that was fine, he knew that, and he didn't want to take up too much of my 'invaluable' time, but would I like a bar of chocolate? And then he presented me with this candy bar, only it was a triangle, not like the ones in Tennessee."

"So?"

"So nothing."

"I still don't get how—"

"I read the Deirdre Bair biography, and she tells about Beckett going to the 1964 World's Fair, and then I remembered the man on the bench and just combined it. The fact from the book and my memory." At this point, Corrine realized she'd never be able to tell even her girlfriends about the day it rained fish.

"I think you need to buy a skirt." Annie was of the Shopping as Therapy school. When the going gets tough, the tough go shopping. "A straight gray-flannel skirt, pearl earrings, and he'll have to take you seriously."

"She doesn't need a skirt, she needs a divorce," said Jill.

"All Corrine needs—" began Elena.

Corrine looked on in silence as the girls reorganized her life for her: Jill adamant, Annie practical, Elena thoughtful. She smiled at the toast crumbs around Annie's mouth, the eyeliner Jill never could get straight. Elena's eyes, half closed, browsing inward, seemed to be searching for ghosts. A red silk blouse was tucked loosely into a red silk skirt. Her lips now hid the extra front tooth she normally displayed in a tortured halfsmile. Her thin hair hung within an inch of her invalid-white shoulders like long dark tinsel. She was a real radabarbara, the most beautiful woman Corrine had ever known.

She tried to imagine life in jail—one cell for her girl-friends, one for Michael and herself. It would be per-fect. A glass of burgundy, a sprig of sweet tea olive, and this argument, forever insoluble, forever open, shut, opened again, to keep them going. Life in jail, life on Mars, with them would be somehow complete. Put there by nothing so ordinary as a spaceship, something as mystical as a parking ticket.

Corrine was five. She and her sister and their little Ten-nessee mom were on a ferryboat crossing the English Channel. It had been raining their whole vacation. They were eating dinner, in a room full of people eating dinner, and her peas kept sliding across her plate and her plate kept sliding across the table. The only thing keeping it from falling into her lap was a protective silver bar, designed for this purpose, running around the perimeter of the table. Corrine, to this day, has always held England responsible for the instability in her life, the kind of insta-bility brought on by peas on a plate in a boat on rough waters.

There was a commotion and people began leaving their tables, running to the outside deck. Corrine and her sister were allowed to go but were to report back on the double. Her sister had on Corrine's favorite skirt, a sweet affair made out of white dotted Swiss, and as they stepped out onto the deck, into the rain, Corrine remembered bargaining with Jesus for it. If Jesus would allow her to borrow the skirt from time to time, she, Corrine, would be happy to do things for *him* from time to time. Outside, grown-ups were looking up, but Corrine couldn't see anything. Then a tiny fish, no bigger than a cat's eye, fell on her brand new patent leather shoes. Then another, and another. She'd seen goldfish before, but these were different. She looked up to where everyone was pointing and saw something and stood still. The sky was raining fish. For an instant, she forgot herself. She forgot about her peas and her mother's dictum. She forgot about her shoes and Jesus and her sister's white dotted Swiss. She stared straight at the sky and held her breath, too stunned to feel anything like wonder.

Rembrandt's Bones

I am sitting here at Stuckey's in the little north Florida town where I grew up, still trying to figure out what to do with a dead girl's midterm. Yesterday, I was in my Chicago apartment trying to figure out the same thing when Mother called to tell me about Opal. I drove straight through.

"Coffee?" the waitress asks, handing me an orange menu.

"A Coke, please."

"All's we have is RC."

"RC's good."

They call it Catholic Coke here, though I am careful not to call it that myself. There are few sights uglier than that of a person who, having been raised in the South, returns after a twenty-year absence in New York, Chicago, or Los Angeles and tries to fit back in. It's like watching a gorilla try to play a CD on a record player. There is a double remove—not only have you lost the grace of knowing how to use the current equipment, you have devolved into an entirely other, if related, species.

I take a look out the window. Matchstick pines line both sides of the highway. Outfitted in kudzu, they form two quiet columns of sleepy marching bears, a poor man's parade. This is the old Florida, the real Florida. Women carry pocketbooks, men eat hamburger meat. People here do not take aspirin, they take a tablet.

I gave the midterm on Wednesday. Last night, one of my students committed suicide. "Right after *Cheers*," one of the campus cops was quoted as saying.

What do you do with a dead girl's midterm?

Opal would have known.

Opal Whiteside was a woman of reason, something absent in the tender history of my own monkey family. She wore pink slacks and Arpège. Instead of cookbooks, she kept an entire set of the Encyclopædia Britannica propped on the kitchen counter, ready for action. A cloud of hair spray and intelligence followed her wherever she went, as I did, through all my wide girlhood, traipsing behind like a dog without a clue. Opal Whiteside was a beautiful woman who had all the answers, and I was a plain girl with a lot of questions.

"Where do you go when you die?" I asked her once.

"You go straight to Miami Beach, order Chinese, and wait for all eternity."

"Is it good?"

"Terribly good. In Miami, there is no need for MSG."

"Then what?"

"Then you make love with the delivery boy."

"Is it good?"

"Terribly good. In Miami, boys talk in bed."

"What do they say?"

"They say *moo goo gai pan.*"

Sundays after church, whenever she could wrench me out of Mother's beautiful sugar-free arms, Opal would drive me out here, to Stuckey's, to drink Cokes, try on lipsticks, and talk about death and sex. Over the years, I have come to think of these episodes as our red-vinyl-booth sessions—like Elvis's Sun sessions, or the Owen Bradley sessions of Patsy Cline. Opal and I were trying to work things out.

"According to Camus, there is but one truly serious philosophical problem, and that is?" Opal's bible was *The Myth of Sisyphus.*

I remember the lipsticks, spread out on the table before me. Candy Cane Pink. Cherry Sunset. Ruby Romance. It was that time in life when any choice you made was the perfect choice.

"Suicide," I said, smiling, my eyes on the Cherry Sunset.

Besides Camus, what Opal talked a lot about was bad sex. I didn't know Camus from Camay. I was eight years old at the time and yet to become accustomed to bad sex, so I would just look at her and smile, thrilling to the red rings around my Coke straw.

"Have you decided yet?" The waitress stands poised, hunched over her order pad like a mother eagle.

"Can I ask? Do you have the salmon croquettes today?"

"I'll check with the cook."

Here is another thing I know but pretend not to. One of the local delights the menu boasts of is the salmon croquettes. They are offered with the parenthetical proviso WHEN IN SEASON. Now I know they make their salmon croquettes with canned salmon, as do I, as do the insane. Not even Martha Stewart is nutty enough to make salmon croquettes with fresh salmon. They're not like crab cakes, where the fresher the crab is, the better. The whole point of salmon croquettes is what you put on them. Look up *croquette* in the dictionary and you'll see: "A desire for tartar sauce."

The waitress returns to tell me. I am in luck. The croquettes are fresh today.

I flatten out the girl's midterm to the right of my knife and fork and iron it down with the palm of my hand, thinking, We've had a long ride, it may be hungry. The whole trip down it sat on the seat beside me, quiet, like a passenger.

I was sitting at my kitchen table yesterday morning when Mother called. I pushed down the toast.

She said it was pineapple night when it happened and they were on the pinochle cake. At least that's what I thought she said. Opal Whiteside was my girlhood hero. If Proust is correct, if objects do indeed have a life all their own, I understand the sudden lean my kitchen took to the left.

It was her heart, Mother said. Dropped dead at the card table in front of God and everybody, seventy-six years of age, never once touched her cake. "Shame," added Mother philosophically. Death, the Lutheran consequence of never having gotten into the habit—well, honey, had she?—of cleaning her plate. Feeling the need to compete with Opal's news, Mother checked off her own list of maladies, one by one, like potential party guests. Seems a certain Dr. Themo, the latest in a long line of witch doctors Mother has subsidized over the years, cured her glaucoma.

"And I can see pretty well," she said.

"What do you mean pretty well?" I said.

"It's a little funny in the one eye."

She applied for a library card for the visually impaired. Mother is not one to mope. Books on tape, that sort of thing. *The Clan of the Cave Bear* was checked out, so she got *Les Miserables.* Indications were she was driving all over town.

"I only go places I know where I'm going, honey. Please don't use the 'f' word."

"It's against the law, Mother. Blind people driving is against the law."

"I am not blind, Deborah Louise. I told you, I am impaired."

Mother was knee deep in seaweed and psychics long before they were popular. "Science is not as smart as it thinks it is!" she likes to say. But she comes by her herbalness genuinely enough. Hospital doctors are why six of her children died in infancy—two sets of twins and two regular babies. They lie in a pretty cemetery in Tampa out by a big lake, buried in little glass cylinders like the pneumatic tubes at a drive-up bank, six silver circles in the ground. As it turned out, she wound up with just the two of us: my sister the Homecoming Queen and me, the heartless academic.

"You sure, honey, you want to drive down?"

"Yes, Mother. You know Chicago at this time of year. One of my students committed—"

"You don't have to tell *me* about the weather in Chicago, Miss Priss. I was *there.* I nearly froze my patootie off, and it was July! Don't tell *me.* Anyplace it gets dark in the squat middle of the day—you *are* taking those sunshine tablets?"

"Yes, Mother."

"Don't con me, kiddo. I spent good money—"

"Mother. Sweetheart. I am."

But she was off. Seasonal affective disorder, the movie. Her voice caught, sputtered, even choked from time to time, but in the end it always kicked in. It was a good engine. Dr. Themo this, Dr. Themo that. Dr. Themo and his Egyptian water therapy. Dr. Themo and the foxglove, the shark cartilage, the cauliflower tea. It was Dr. Themo who revolutionized the medical world's thinking on the pancreas . . . no, the pituitary . . . no—

"The gizmo that regulates, you know, honey, the thingamajig."

"Kidney?"

"That's it."

Elvis would still be alive had he taken Dr. Themo's advice. Eat nothing yellow. Drink nothing brown. Take a walk on the sunny side of the street.

"Is it money?"

"No, Mother, it isn't money."

"Is it a man? Because if it's a man—"

"No, Mother, it isn't a man."

"Only one reason I can think of a grown woman'll confine herself to the inside of an automobile car and drive willingly in it for close to one thousand miles of gray Yankee highway, and that is a man reason."

"Mother, please."

"My ears are wide open. Talk."

I didn't feel like talking about my student, acquainted as I already was with Mother's views on suicide. *Suicide, honey, is a matter of glands.* This, the glandular argument, was Mother's standard response not only to suicide but to any ugly subject she did not wish to address: my father, my choice of attire, the 1968 Democratic Convention. *Your potassium falls off, way off, and before you can say snap-crackle-pop, you think there is no God.* Mother is a forward-looking person who believes in taking an active approach to life. *A glass of iron tonic and one of my broccoli burgers and I'll show you the meaning of life!*

Mother's second argument was of a more spiritual nature. Life, for Mother, is a dinner invitation from the Host of Hosts—who for Mother is a tall good-looking white man approximately her age with impeccable table manners and a Buick. *You wouldn't turn down an invitation from the best-looking man in the universe, now, would you?*

So instead of talking about my student, I gave Mother the news about my grant. The funding had finally come through.

"Isn't that something, sweetheart? I am so proud of you. You know your sister got her interview. She's going on *Wheel of Fortune!*"

My sister had already done *The Joker's Wild* a few years back. In pregame practice she won eighteen grand and a trip for two to Puerto Vallarta, but on the real thing she guessed Bette Davis when they asked who *Mommie Dearest* was about. Every Christmas the video was brought out and we would sit and watch my sister lose over and over again, Mother's applesauce cake fresh out of the oven and warm on our laps. You couldn't play the tape too many times for Mother. It was a great victory to have a daughter on TV.

"You pack those sunshine tablets, Missy. Put them in your pocketbook so's you have them *with*. Those are not for cure, please remember. Those are for maintenance!"

We did not go to doctors, growing up. We went to the backs of people's houses. I knew how to spell *poultice* before I knew what a polka dot was. We'd pull up into somebody's carport where baby food jars spewing starter shoots of herbal everything were arranged into meaningful mandalas under pointy Spanish bayonets, the tips of which were festively ornamented with pink cups cut out from Styrofoam egg cartons. A devil boy around eight or nine would be there throwing a basketball up against the carport wall, over and over again, to the sound of his own nether heart, the sound an incantation of tin. Often there would be a monkey.

Once there was a monkey and a rabbit, a little spider monkey that wore a diaper. The monkey and the rabbit lived together in a big cage just to the right of the carport, in a side yard littered with eyes of God made from cheap colored yarn. I stepped out of the car and our eyes locked, mine and the monkey's. The monkey jumped down on top of the rabbit, grabbed its ears for reins, and rode his reluctant pony around the cage once and then again, faster. He threw back his tiny head, shot me a look, and laughed like Satan. The monkey's name was Mims.

"There was no monkey."

Every time I mention the monkey to Mother, she tells me I have a vivid imagination. Yesterday was no exception.

"Deborah Louise, you have a vivid imagination."

"It belonged to Myrtelene," I told her. "Myrtelene and her little son, Bumpy."

"Myrtelene didn't have any son."

"Nephew, then."

"Nephew neither."

"He was in the carport. He was bouncing a basketball off the carport wall. He was like a gnome."

"Myrtelene didn't have any carport."

Unlike me, Mother does not find the past interesting because, in my version of it, she always comes out looking a little kooky—hence my nickname for her, Major Kookybird. She thinks I am criticizing and who can blame her? What mother in these days of mother blame wouldn't?

"There was no monkey."

"You're right, Mama Bear." I told her this because I

love my mother with all my heart and all my soul. I repeated after her, "There was no monkey."

But there was.

And inside the house was the lady.

The lady had me put on a slip approximately ten years too big for me. It went all the way to the floor, trailing behind like a poor girl's wedding dress. The lady told me the Lord was my shepherd, I shall not want. Jalousie windows rattled in their slats. She placed something heavy and warm on my chest.

"Put your head inside and breathe deep. We're going to get that Devil out of you."

It was a pillowcase filled with boiled onions.

Myrtelene, Imogenia, Randy-Ann: each had her own idea about health and nutrition, and no matter how kooky, they all stayed well within the good boundaries of homeopathic panaceas—beet juice and the Bible, iron tonic and the colonic. The thing is, though, that what you want when you are sick and you are a little kid is what everybody else has got, a real doctor like you see on TV. You want Dr. Kildare in a bleached-white lab coat, a silver stethoscope with a Windex shine gleaming from his beautiful scrubbed neck. You want medicine— liquid, nasty, and red. You want wooden tongue depressors thrown away after each use, white surgical gloves thrown away after each use, paper hospital gowns, paper shoes, disinfected everything. You dream of being given a shot.

Not broccoli and Ben-Gay. Not Mentholatum Deep-Heat Rub smeared on a sanitary napkin and tied around your neck when you had a sore throat.

Opal put a stop to that one. She even got me to a real doctor once with Mother's reluctant okay. Yet had things been any other way I never would have met my monkey. One thing I know: I owe everything to the monkey.

The day I met him galloping around his cage on the back of that bunny, I acquired a layer of consciousness I do not believe I could have reached any other way. Look at me, the monkey seemed to say. Look at what I am doing, riding this bunny. Do you think this is a good thing or a bad thing?

I had to think.

Surely the bunny could not be having much fun. So, bad thing. The monkey was clearly having more fun than he should be having. The monkey, in fact, looked as though he would've known what to do with a whip. Really bad thing.

On the other hand, I know bunnies. Bunnies are strong. Bunnies bite. The body weight of that bunny was twice that of the little spider monkey. That bunny could have kicked cowboy-monkey ass if need be. So. Maybe the bunny was having fun too. Bunnies get bored. Maybe the bunny even felt a certain amount of gratitude toward the monkey for coming up with the idea in the first place—for if one thing was clear, the whole thing was the monkey's idea.

I took that monkey home with me that day—in my mind, that is—and he is still with me today. He accompanies me to record stores—Hoagy Carmichael for me, Ween for the monkey—and to the movies. Romantic comedies are about all I can take these days—give me Meg Ryan anything—but it's Tarantino and Tarantino knockoffs for the monkey. Grocery shopping: chicken again or Chilean sea bass? Raisin or sesame? Whole or skim? Even at the voting booth: Nixon? Bad thing. Carter, Clinton? Good thing, good thing. When I read in the paper about kids who kill their parents or people who blow up other people, I think, There goes somebody who never had a monkey. Or maybe they had a purely bad monkey. I lucked out. Because, although he nags me from time to time since it does take me forever and a day to make the smallest of decisions, I love my monkey.

But there is another side to him.

I am not dying of leukemia nor do I have a child who is dying of leukemia. Money is not exactly no object, but neither is it a big issue. I love my job. And although my boyfriend could be a bit more attentive, he is neither under federal indictment nor attempting to make a living by playing a musical instrument. Life is interesting. Friends are kind and then thoughtless and then kind again, and they make good company. Love is disappointing and then it isn't. Nothing happens and then something does. It's a pretty three-o'clock life. But sometimes, deep at night, my monkey will wake me up, wild-eyed, his spider-hair arms around my neck, and I feel a strangling. On these occasions it is not the monkey but me who asks, Is this a good thing or a bad thing? To which there is never any reply. And then I wake up.

I realize I am sitting in the very booth Opal and I sat in during our red-vinyl-booth sessions. The plastic's peeling off the same place it was peeling off twenty years ago, where the father's head goes. It's the VO 5, still a seller.

The funeral is tomorrow. I fudged a bit to Mother about my estimated time of arrival so as to have a chance to perform the necessary sea change. Opal's funeral coincided with spring break at my college, where Mondays, Wednesdays, and Fridays I teach art history to the completely disinterested, dispensing Rembrandt and the Renaissance part-time (code word for free). I am giddy, having driven straight through from Chicago on twenty-one hours of, as Mother said, gray Yankee highway. I had decided to drive down rather than fly; I knew I could use all the nothingness those twenty-one hours of highway hypnosis were happy to provide.

I dig in my purse for Mother's sunshine tablets, take two, and look out the window. It is a squat shoestring

Florida town. The air is bruised and full of contradiction. There is grace and rot and night-blooming jasmine—a trace of the ancient dame and her soldier son. It is the kind of place where, before the day closes, you are likely to hear the word *poppycock*.

This is a word town.

It was Opal's love of words that gave me the idea of being a teacher in the first place. Our red vinyl sessions were my first vocabulary lessons. Every Sunday, Opal would ask me the same question: "What is the most beautiful word in the English language?" And every week, in order to demonstrate my devotion, I tried out every single word an eight-year-old girl living a trailer-park life could brag of: *sentience, ambidextrous, ennui.* Somehow they were never enough. But there was one time, I remember, I was sure I had her.

"Celerity," I said, holding my breath. It was the only word in *Pride and Prejudice* I had to look up.

"Celerity," said Opal. "Rapidity of motion or action. From the French '*celer*,' meaning swift. Celerity is nice, but I was thinking of something else, something simple. I was thinking *next.*"

I gave her the most intelligent *huh?* I could muster. I was incredulous—the quality or state of disbelief, from the French *credu*, meaning crudball, meaning numbskull, meaning me.

"Think about it," Opal said.

You can bet I thought about it. I loved this big beautiful brainy woman with all my heart, as only a plain eight-year-old girl can. While other kids were in the yard loud with kickball, I spent entire evenings in the kitchen reading the dictionary, reading everything, believing then as I believe today that the exact right word can change the world. I searched day and night for that word, the word that would make this woman sit up and take notice, the one word this woman did not know.

"Why do people answer the doorbell?" she asked me.

"To see who it is."

"Beyond the mere Pavlovian response to, as you say, Deborah Louise, see who it is, there is something else. A certain expectation—"

"It might be Ed McMahon. It might be a million bucks."

"It needn't take that form."

"What do you mean, form?"

"I mean it needn't take the pecuniary form you have just so adroitly pointed out, Deborah Louise."

I knew *pecuniary*. I knew *adroit*. What I didn't know was what this woman was talking about.

"Why don't we just kill ourselves, Deborah Louise? This instant?"

"I don't know." I said, ready to. To add insult to injury, Opal had informed me that the hero of *Pride and Prejudice* was not Lydia but Elizabeth.

"Think."

I was thinking. Nothing.

"What did you learn at the end of *Pride and Prejudice*?"

"Darcy wasn't that stuck up."

"You read to the end of the whole book just for that?"

I did not tell her I read to the end of the whole book just to find one word she did not know—that recently witnessed exercise in pointlessness.

Opal tried on her patient voice. "What was your favorite part of the whole book?" she asked me.

"Lydia when she gets Wickham."

"So once she gets Wickham, once Lydia comes home married, why keep reading?"

Opal clearly had landed on Mars and forgotten to call home, so I had to celebrate the obvious for her. "To see what happens!"

"To see what happens—"

I said it. "Next."

"Same with life. People stick around, they answer the door, they answer the phone, they go to Las Vegas, they get up in the morning. They want to see what might happen."

"But your Cousin Alma—"

"One does eventually grow weary waiting for the glorious to arrive, Deborah Louise. Please pass the sugar."

Opal's Cousin Alma was married to my second cousin J. W., and when J. W. died, Alma showed up at the funeral with a lady-pink pistol and shot him five times in his open coffin before they could get the gun away from her. They couldn't figure out what to charge her with.

I passed Opal the sugar.

Opal believed in the power of sugar. She put sugar in her Coke. She liked to sprinkle it on top and watch it fizz down into the brown until it disappeared. She told me that when she died I should just fill her coffin up with sugar, as she was uncertain of its availability in the next world. "A world without sugar, baby doll," she told me, "is no world whatsoever."

While Mother raisined our oatmeal with niacin tablets and wheat-germed our milk, Opal baked us sugar cakes and sugar cookies, deep-fried us sugar doughnuts. Her iced tea was famous because she didn't brew it, she distilled it. She let it sit out on her back porch in a big tin pitcher all afternoon long, three cups of sugar strong. Hummingbirds came. She called it her Florida champagne and served it in pretty colored, tin glasses, and when you drank it your head swam off. Once, when she heard Mother had served us carrot cake for dessert—the first carrot cake in the state of Florida, Mother would have you know—Opal church-keyed open a brand new can of Hershey's chocolate syrup and stuck in a straw. She handed it to me and let me go, saying, "Carrots is not dessert."

It was Opal who saved my life the night of the Snowflake Princess Dance.

There I sat, furious and forlorn on my little pink bed in my little pink bedroom, up to my princess neck in cotton-candy chiffon. Mother had not gone soft on her no makeup commandment. No lipstick, no nothing. Not even for a Snowflake Princess. I sat on my bed waiting for my date, a good-looking blond boy with no personality, riffling through *Seventeen* magazine advice—MAYONNAISE! THE POOR WOMAN'S MOISTURIZER!—when all of a sudden there was someone behind me. I looked up and there stood Opal.

She said, "Close your eyes and stick out your tongue. This worked for Cleopatra and it'll work for you." She dabbed something like salt on my tongue, and in seconds my cheeks and lips were rose red and stayed that way the whole princess night.

"Arsenic," she told me. "Just don't overdo it."

Then she stood back and drank a Coke. Opal happened to be one of those women who knew how to look when she drank a Coke straight out of the bottle. She was as tall as a man. She had on her famous Loretta Young skirt, navy blue with white polka dots, womanly but full of girl. She threw back her head—you could smell the Gulf of Mexico suddenly in the room—and took a long, slow drink, the bottle of Coke trumpeting skyward. The whole room leaned. She looked like Louis Armstrong summoning home the chariots. She looked like Dom Pérignon when he discovered champagne. When he said, "Oh my God, I'm drinking the stars."

"The salmon croquettes," says the waitress, arriving with my plate. "Will there be anything else?"

"May I please get another RC?"

"Most certainly may."

Where the restaurant part ends, the gift shop begins. And straight ahead, at the end of my line of sight, I see— over past the saltwater taffy, the JFK key chains, all manner of highway toys—a satisfied-looking bird with a pointed beak, dipping its head down into a plastic martini glass in perpetuity, up, down, up, down.

I open the girl's midterm and begin to read.

It is a D-minus, which I can hardly send to the grieving parents with a note about what a great et cetera she was. She wasn't.

I could change the D to a B the way it was done in high school, but even the D-minus was a gift. She didn't identify any of the fifty slides, and she only responded to one of the four essay questions. That one response was mildly interesting, but it was shot through with inaccuracies: 1649 is just not in the sixteenth century; I wish it were.

If I could lay my hands on the same green Pilot pen I

used to grade the thing, maybe I could change the minus to a plus. But a D-plus? Wouldn't that be like pinning a sequin on a rat's ass, Bette Davis's famous line from some old movie about what it would be like to compliment Joan Crawford?

I read somewhere about a suicide's mother who pushed past police to her dead son's bathroom just to get the hair out of his hairbrush. Wouldn't this girl's mother, likewise, want every last thing, even a D-minus midterm? At least it was in her handwriting. Mightn't the handwriting have the effect on the mother of an old love letter, one you keep and read over and over again, not for the words but for the pleasure of the sight of it, the look of it, the arc and fall of the *this* and the *that*?

Or would the effect be the opposite? Might there be something in the girl's scribble that would act as an accusation? The very recognition of the hand, the way the girl made her capital A, might well produce a stab instead of a solace, wounding the mother every time she came across it, either purposefully or by chance, in a scrapbook, a file cabinet, a loose kitchen drawer.

I can't just throw it away, pretend it doesn't exist, thereby solving my dilemma.

The waitress returns with my RC. To my horror, she sets it down straight on my student's midterm.

"Sorry," she says, seeing my undisguised distress.

"Oh. No problem," I say.

But I am not quick enough, and because of the moisture from the bottom of the glass, the writing begins to bleed.

"I'll get more napkins."

"That's okay," I tell the waitress. "I've got it."

She looks at me, turns, and goes back to her station.

The moment is oddly emotional. I have spoken too sharply, feeling an insane desire to keep the girl's handwriting safe. Safe from what? The waitress? A napkin? It makes no sense. All I know is I want the waitress to stay away. I do not want her to see. I do not want her to ask me what it is I'm reading here. I do not want to have to say, "Oh, nothing." I don't think I could say, "Oh, nothing."

The course was a survey in art history. The Venus of Willendorf through Karen Finley in a sixteen-week spin. The history of art on a yellow 78.

The class was riding high. I'd marched them up the Carolingian, down the Merovingian, and into the animal style. Gals fell silent before the cloisonné, the panther clasp, a world before buttons. Guys paid mute respect to the seriously enameled handles of war. When I put up a slide from *The Book of Kells* the whole room took a deep breath, even Randall Huddleston III. Inlaid gold? Think of it, the look on his face said, I mean in today's market. A newfound respect for art and artists alike suddenly took hold of him. You could see *The Book of Kells,* the *Hypnerotomachia Poliphili,* the duc de Berry's *Très riches heures,* the whole world's store of priceless incunabula, all melting down into a pool of gold, and Randy with his mother's good cake pan collecting the hot liquid, cooling it into heavy gold rounds, suitcasing it off to Switzerland where it would sit in a fabulous honeymoon suite and wait pretty as a wedding cake for him and his new bride, Michelle Pfeiffer.

The girl sat in the back of the room. She never said a word, never raised a hand, never took the first note.

She was the only thing alive in that classroom.

She never even bought the text. The only book she ever brought to class was a beat-up copy of *The Idiot.* She sat there silently every Monday, Wednesday, and Friday from 10:00 to 10:50 A.M. reading her Dostoevsky, with all the attention of a lover. She ignored us as hard as she could. She ignored me, she ignored Albrecht Dürer, she ignored Randall Huddleston III. She sat, in fact, as far from Randall Huddleston III as it was possible to sit, saving herself for Prince Myshkin.

I didn't even know what a cutter was. When my own personal brand of self-flagellation surfaces, I deny myself the Moët and make do with Korbel. When I want to flirt with death, I say no for a month to Princess Borghese and go down the moisturizer ladder to Clinique.

This girl cut herself.

The one and only time I can remember that she ever even looked up, we were on Rembrandt.

"Part of the success of Rembrandt's luminous brown," I was saying, "is due to his use of pulverized human bone." I could tell the idea struck her. Bone going to powder.

She looked up at me. And I think she wanted to know if that was a good thing or a bad thing—using human bones. I had never really thought about it. I heard myself talking, I listened to myself speak. But there was nothing about that.

What I said was, "Next slide, please." *Carceri d'Invenzione.* A series of fantastic imaginary prisons by Giovanni Battista Piranesi. Though never constructed, these are the finest examples of his architectural renderings. Begun in 1745, reworked in 1781.

"Lady?"

There is a boy standing at my table. He is wearing a suit. Somehow the suit is ten years too old for him. It takes me a minute. Me. I'm the lady.

"You want your game? Ours don't have all the things in it."

He is pointing to a little wood triangle, one of those highway toys Stuckey's offers for the stimulation of the long-distance traveler. There are short orange pegs sticking up out of it.

"Eddie. Over here. This minute."

And the little guy is gone. Reseated with his mother, he bows his head, seemingly benumbed by years and years of never getting anything his way. The boy and his mother are dressed in black, poor people's black, on their way to a funeral. Even the mother's black barrettes, placed square and equidistant from the part, seem to know how to behave at a restaurant, at a funeral, at this and all of life's other slender occasions.

"Hand me my pocketbook." The mother is up. "And Eddie. I said don't put sugar on your french fries." The mother breezes by me to pay her bill, leaving the smell of poverty and brilliantine in her wake. I feel the little guy looking at me, looking at me hard, so I glance up.

He is holding the silver-topped sugar canister high above a mountain of french fries, and he is looking at me. I think he wants to know. Would this be a good thing or a bad thing?

And at this moment my monkey comes to me, saying that to send the D-minus to the dead girl's mother would be a bad thing. But wait. What if I were to take what the girl wrote and type it up in the form of an essay? She didn't write much, but what she did say—basically questioning Rembrandt's use of human bones, even to make what is arguably great art—would make a perfectly respectable essay, something Camus himself might enjoy. I could type it up on my computer in MLA style: her name, my name, course title, date, one-inch margins, and a nice letter-gothic face. (And may I say what a lovely century it is, since this particular solution in any other century would be out of the question.) I'll fix all the little things. I'll put 1649 back into the seventeenth century, I'll put the *d* back into "Rembrant," and voilà! Then, instead of the easy tenured-professor adjectives—*interesting, insightful,* and the ever popular *yes*—I'll make real comments in the margins and a detailed end comment about her powers of observation. And it will be the truth, the part about her powers of observation. I'll title it "Rembrandt's Bones" and I'll give it a B-plus. Okay, what the fucking fuck, I'll give it an A.

And this will be a small thing, a very small thing, but a good thing.

The midterm itself? It *is* a document. I can't just throw it away. And then I realize—and please remember it is me this time and not my monkey who gets the idea—Opal will need something to read in the afterlife. I figure she'll have an open casket. Opal knew even dead she'd be the best-looking woman there.

I look up. The boy lingers, waiting, sugar canister held high, and it seems to me at this moment that the whole wide world is on its way to a funeral. I look past the little guy to the Rebel flags and GooGoo Clusters, the alligator ashtrays and JFK penny banks, the wooden back scratchers with faces of jokey men on the backside, the IF

YOUR HEART'S NOT IN DIXIE GET YOUR ASS OUT license plates, the rows of ceramic kittens, the stacks of ceramic plates—to this whole pecan divinity. I look at the boy and raise my Coke high, toast his sugar experiment.

He looks at me once, twice, then goes. I watch the little guy pour.

"Is it good?" I ask, and he nods, looking at me, ridiculous now, with my Coke sky high. I must look like the top half of the Statue of Liberty, only a little loaded. And so we sit, this little guy and I, our hearts beating wildly. We sit and wait and see. See how much trouble we are in for, because this time we know we are both of us going to get it. We wait to see what the waitress will say, or the manager of this crazy ceramic dream. See what a woman with barrettes like that might do. What in the world might happen next.

About the Author

Phyllis Moore's short stories have appeared in *Redbook*, *The Georgia Review*, *The Mississippi Review*, *The Apalachee Quarterly*, and the *Michigan Quarterly Review*. She has been awarded numerous arts council grants from the states of Florida and Illinois and currently teaches writing in the MFA program at The School of the Art Institute in Chicago.